-1-

It was a crisp spring morning in the year 1850 when Jean came into the world, it was one week later when Paul arrived. Jean was born with dark hair and green eyes, Paul had blue eyes and tight, curly, blond hair. Jean had an older brother named Pierre that was sick with tuberculosis at the time of Jeans birth. No one was more excited about the birth of Jean, and equally excited at the birth of Paul just a short week after, than Pierre was. He thought of all the things that he could do with them, teach them the things that he had learned in his eleven years of life. This made Pierre feel important, he would revel in this and forget about his illness. He was more excited about being an older brother than he was about having a younger one. However, it was not meant to be, death took Pierre when Jean and Paul were two months old. Fortunately for the two boys they were too young, they had no memory of Pierre, they only knew what their parents had told them. They visited the graves of their family members often, always paying a special visit to the grave of Pierre. Their families had known each other for generations, delighting in the joys of one another's lives, and sharing in the suffering of one another's losses. Their fathers worked together at the foundry. Their grandfathers were both dairy farmers. The beautiful, green pastures around the village were ideal for raising dairy cows. As the two boys grew up, they were always together, an inseparable pair. The two of them were not yet born when a smallpox epidemic had ravaged their village back in the 1840's, but they grew up with the results of it all around them. Many of their friends and family had died. Fortunately, their parents had not. It was due to their care and guidance that Jean and Paul excelled at everything they tried to do. The two of them did very well in school, and they never missed Mass on Sunday. The two were known around town as good-hearted boys, pranksters, but good-hearted. They were given pastries and sweets from the local baker quite often. The old baker, having never had children of his own, and having had lost his wife to the smallpox in 1842, treated Jean and Paul as if they were his children, he cared for them dearly. Jean and Paul would often go fishing in the river Meuse, they would give their catch to the baker and other neighbors that were perhaps, not as fortunate. They loved to pick lavender from the field and give it to everyone. They found the fresh purple bulbs to be absolutely, irresistible. Almost every home in the village had fresh lavender in the window. Everyone had high expectations for the two boys, especially their parents. The boy's marks in school warranted such expectations. Jean and Paul wanted to be doctors more than anything. Perhaps the sickness and death of Jean's brother helped them to make up their minds. They did not like to see anything suffer, or even hear about it, especially people. Watching Jean's brother die a little bit more every day, and not being able to do anything about it, hurt both families. They were grateful that Jean and Paul did not have to suffer that experience. The two of them were such gentle souls, it would have pained them deeply, more than could be imagined. There was never a better time to grow up in the village of Briey, a happy, peaceful place in the north-east of France. There was plenty of work to be had, the region was known for its steel and dairy industries. On the weekends the two families would often get together along with many of the other families from the village and go out into the fields for a picnic. There was often a pig roasting, the smell would fill the air and mix with the fragrance of lavender, it was the image of heaven. They would play football until the sun had went down. Then they would kick the ball back and forth, while lagging behind their parents. There were plenty of young girls in the village, about the same age as Jean and Paul, but the realization of the completion that is brought about by a union between the two they still did not understand, so they resorted to playing pranks on each other, as children of that age often do. Sometimes they would take a carriage into Metz to see a show. The boys always liked going to Metz, it was the biggest town they had ever seen, as far as they knew, it was the biggest town in the whole world. There were sights there that they could not see in Briey, and their favorite was the cathedral of St. Stephen's, with its massive array of stained glass. It was as if looking at the world through a different pair of eyes. While there they would always pray for their families and for Jean's older brother. They also loved the opera house, although they had never attended an opera. It was simply the joy of their being youths at that time. Everything they saw was gathered into their minds as something spectacular. Nothing bothered Jean, and even less bothered Paul. They seemed to be immune to hatred and dishonesty, that was a trait specific to others. Caste meant nothing to them, they had no sense of hierarchy. When they arrived home, Paul asked his father if God was looking over them and taking care of Jean's brother. "Certainly, God looks over us all." His father replied. Not sure if he even believed that himself, but mankind could not exist without hope. Jean and Paul believed it, even if no one else did. God gave such hope, and these boys believed that with all their hearts. What else was there? Their personalities became more defined with every passing day. They loved to perform pranks on any unsuspecting neighbors, but it was always just for fun, and they always let their neighbors know that they did it. Their pranks were always meant to bring surprising joy, not fear or disgust. Throughout their years in primary school they did well, not extraordinary, but well. These were very formative years for these two, they were still discovering who they were, and who everyone else was, but they had already discovered their dependency on each other. At the age of twelve Paul started developing a crush for a girl in their class. Her name was Marie. She had the prettiest dark brown eyes, and the longest, blackest hair that Paul had ever seen. He was intrigued. Still being youthful enough to not take anything too serious, their relationship was not to get off the ground, but they remained friends, and Paul's crush continued. At the same time Jean had developed a crush of his own, Miss Bardin, their teacher. Miss Bardin was able to explain the nature of romantic relationships with Jean much better than Marie could with Paul, in fact, Marie had no idea either. The two of them, Jean and Paul, shared this information back and forth, neither of them really knowing what they were talking about. They would go down to the river Meuse after school and go fishing. That is when they would fill each other in on who they liked, who they did not, and who they just did not think about at all. One day, while down at the river, Paul said that he was not feeling well, then he started vomiting uncontrollably. Jean ran to Paul's house and got Paul's father, he would know what to do. Paul's father raced down to the river, picked him up and carried him home, Jean following behind the whole time. A doctor was called, he diagnosed Paul with a bad fever, but he did not know what brought it on. Every day after school Jean would go to Paul's house to see how his friend was doing. After three days there was no break in the fever. Jean went by himself to the river Meuse, there he sat down on its shore and cried. He cried for his older brother that he didn't get a chance to know, but most of all he cried for Paul. Without him he did not even know what to do, all their dreams would unitedly disappear. They were closer than brothers and the thought of losing him broke his heart all up inside. After spending the longest week alone that Jean had ever experienced Paul's fever broke. Paul's mother went to Jean's house to tell them the good news. The words were not completely out of her mouth when Jean ran past his mother and out the front door. He did not stop running until he was at Paul's house. He knocked and yelled for Paul. When Paul's father opened the front door, Jean flew past him and ran to Paul's room.

"Your awake!" Jean shouted as he ran to Paul's bed with his eyes full of tears. "Everyone at school is asking about you. I miss you. Are you okay?" Jean cried. Paul could not understand him through his sobbing, but he knew exactly what Jean meant.

"I'm fine, much better anyway."

Jean had never been so scared in his life. He had never been without Paul and the very thought of it sent a fear through his young mind unlike anything he had ever experienced. From that day on Jean took it as his personal responsibility to look after Paul. Paul did not need that, but Jean did. Throughout their years in primary school they became more distinct. Each had his own personality, but the things that divide men amongst themselves, religion, politics, racial barriers, class struggles, and all the other petty squabbles that exist among men were totally absent from their minds. Love united them and left no room for divisive distractions. Primary school was not the start of their education, but a continuation of it. Their parents had always encouraged reading, studying, and preparing themselves for something better. With these two boys it took, they loved to read, study, and find out what made things tick. They finished their training in primary school, they would begin their secondary schooling in the fall. During their summer off they made extra money working on some of the surrounding farms. Fresh dairy products for their families was an extra benefit. They both had uncles that owned the farms that had belonged to their grandfathers. The two of them decided to work for Jean's uncle so that they could still be together. They saved all their money at the encouragement of their fathers. During their time off they would go fishing and have long conversations about nothing important. They were in their early teens now, so sometimes they would talk about girls, sometimes they would talk about medicine, they wanted to be doctors, that had not changed and it was not likely that it ever would. Jean was enthralled with the idea that perhaps his brother could have been saved, and Paul may have never gotten sick. To be able to help people never have to experience these things again, it sounded like magic, but they knew that it could be a reality. They began spending more of their free time at the library and the museum when they went to Metz. Advances in medicine over the past centuries was an incredible feat. They would check out books and take them home and do mock surgeries on each other. They would study these books down to the last detail, then they would quiz each other on what was in the book. Then they would return the book, get another one and do the same thing again. The two boys became very adept at reading, studying, and understanding. Before they were to begin secondary school, their families went to Metz to see a show. Jean and Paul could not have been happier. They visited the University where they were given a guided tour. They fell in love with the place, its level of education, as well as its hands-on training. They left the university and went over to the morgue. They asked the mortician if they could help.

"I don't think that would be a good idea. Where are your parents?"

"They are shopping, we have to meet them at the theatre in two hours."

"I guess it would be all right, for a little while." As the mortician cut into the body he glanced over at Jean and Paul expecting to see them turn away with sour looks on their faces. This, however, was not the case. The two boys looked on in eager anticipation. As internal organs were revealed Jean and Paul would point them out accurately, as well as mentioning anything that may have been visibly wrong with them. The mortician was utterly amazed at these two young boys that could do his job at least as well as he could. They left the morgue, after saying goodbye, and thanking the mortician for letting them observe. They arrived at the theater just before their parents. The play began, but neither Paul nor Jean had any idea what it was about, their minds were far too occupied. On the ride back to Briey their parents asked them how their day went. Jean and Paul broke out into a cacophony of verbiage. After they slowed down enough to make sense to their parents their moms shouted, "You went to a morgue?"

"Yes, there were bodies there and everything. The mortician even let us observe an autopsy."

"You did what?"

"Relax," Paul's father said. "You know that they want to be doctors, they're just preparing themselves for it."

"I agree," Jean's father replied.

The two boys went back in their minds to the excitement of the day. They've studied, they went to the museum, but this was the first time that they had ever seen a medical procedure done on a human body, they loved the experience, knowing that in the future it would serve them well.

-2-

On the first day of secondary school everyone was asked to introduce themselves, give a short biography, and state what it was that they hoped to achieve in life. It seemed to be an odd request, since everyone in the village knew everyone else, but not everyone was close. There were several strange and diverse answers. One kid said he wanted to be a circus performer, one even said he wanted to be a gravedigger because he would always have work, and a cute redhead wanted to be a prostitute because that was what her mommy was. Jean and Paul both said they wanted to be surgeons, Paul said that it was his life's ambition to help people and to save lives. Jean said that his goal was to put the gravedigger out of business. The class erupted with laughter, except for the kid that wanted to be a gravedigger. It could be seen on the teachers face, she was impressed with some answers, others, not too much. It was at this time in their education that the two of them began to excel. Most of their subjects bored them, but they knew that they needed to get high marks in everything. Math was Jeans least favorite, whereas Paul got along well in math. Paul did not like history, or literature. Jean was exceptionally good at these subjects, he had a love for reading that Paul did not. They both loved biology and anatomy, just like it was with everything else, they would always help each other when and where it was needed. Paul maintained a friendship with Marie throughout their school years. When the time came that they were both older, romantic feelings started to get involved, more on the part of Marie than Paul. Jean was the only secondary relationship that Paul afforded himself to have, and it was a kinship of brothers that they both knew could not be broken. Their marks in school were remarkably high, the highest in the class. They understood that if they were to get into the university, they would have to maintain these marks, this only drove them to excel even more. They studied hard and passed, with honors, every test that they took. Their chances of going to the university were looking good, but they would still have to apply and be accepted. They had put off their studies for the upcoming May Day festival. It was traditional to leave a gift at the door of a romantic interest. Neither of them really had one, but Paul went ahead and put a basket of sweets with a bundle of lavender at the doorstep of Marie, it remained anonymous. Jean left the whole gift giving alone, there was no one that he wanted to give anything to, no romantic interest for him at all. He did not really care, his studies were his only interest. On the day of the festival everyone from the village gathered in the field. There was a thrill and much excitement in the air. Everyone was feasting on pork and sweet cakes that were brought out by the old baker. When the actual festivities began Marie was crowned the queen of May Day, she had received the best gift, that was entirely due to Paul's generosity. Later in the evening Marie approached Paul and asked if the basket was from him, he denied that it was, but she deserved it he said. She still did not believe that it was not from him. They sat down under a large black pine and talked for a moment. Paul noticed Jean and a girl from school named Emma underneath a juniper kissing. At that moment Paul felt like that was what he was supposed to do. He gently leaned into Marie and gave her a small kiss on the cheek. He was unwilling to make a move that would indicate something more than he really felt. She was flattered none-the-less. Emma did not care about Jean any more than he cared about her, they were simply happy to have company for the moment. Everything went well. Paul and Jean talked later about what had happened between them and the two girls. Neither had any feelings towards the other, just well wishes. Jean told Paul that he thought that was what they were supposed to do, find a pretty girl, and kiss them. No one took it seriously. School started back the following Monday. Apart from strange looks from Marie and Emma everything continued as it always had. They were nearing the end of secondary school, Paul and Jean could not have been more pleased. They carried on an amateurish relationship with Emma and Marie respectively, one that they never allowed to get too involved. Before they had graduated from secondary school their families took another trip to Metz. Jean and Paul were beside themselves with excitement. They were sure that was where they wanted to go to the university, it was much closer than Paris, and, from what they heard, much safer. There was a better chance of their knowing people in Metz than Paris. University in Metz seemed like the better decision. It was a university of great renown, and it was close to their beloved Briey. They imagined the things that they would learn, the people that they would be able to help. Their motives were completely selfless, even the recognition that would come from being great surgeons sat in their minds as if an albatross around their neck. Their desire to do good outweighed the albatross. On Sunday morning they attended Mass, they praised God for the opportunities that they believed He had sat out before them. They prayed for their families, each other, and the peace of God to be with the world. They hoped that He would help with their education, but they knew that would be up to them, and hard work. Secondary school had finally come to an end. Jean and Paul applied to the university in Metz immediately. Their fathers had gotten work at the foundry for them. They were paid a decent wage, but it was extremely hot work, and dangerous. Steel was molten, cast, and pounded out into sheets, then it would be cut and formed into its various uses. Sparks were constantly flying. They had a newfound respect for their fathers, not as parents, but as men. They did this day in and day out to support their families and to make sure that they would be able to have a good education. It was extremely hot in there and the potential for serious burns and other injuries was a real factor. They worked there for a couple of months before receiving letters of acceptance from the university in Metz. Classes would begin in the summer of 1868. They had saved up quite a bit of money. They decided, with approval from their parents, that they would do a brief excursion to see some of the things, and places that they never had. They said their goodbyes to Emma and Marie, they stopped by the school to say goodbye to Miss Bardin, she was extremely proud of the two boys, they were her more memorable students. A special goodbye to the old baker, and their mom and dad. They did not know when they might be home again, there was a heartfelt goodbye for this very reason.

-3-

Being the first time that they had ever left Briey in

a carriage not on the road to Metz, was somewhat unsettling, but it held out the possibility of excitement, which is what they thought they wanted. They stopped overnight in several small towns and villages; an outpost that sat between Verdun and Mars la Tour, Thiancourt along the Meuse, Bar le Duc, south to St. Dixier. They noticed the similarities between every small town and village. There was always a baker, school, moms and dads, and joys and miseries. Everyone, everywhere, suffered the same losses and experienced the same tribulations. It still did not feel remotely close to home. These were not their bakers, nor their teachers, nor their moms and dads. The similarities were there, but the emotional attachment was not. They left St. Dixier by boat, heading towards Paris. They enjoyed steaming up the river Marne. Neither of them had ever travelled by boat, although they spent a better part of their childhood on the banks of the Meuse, this was a new and thrilling experience. The captain was an old mariner, looked as if he had been for centuries. As it turned out he was quite amiable. He wore a pair of waders to protect his legs from the sea spray. He wore a jacket over the top of a red sleeping flannel, the jacket appeared to be made from the heaviest canvas Jean or Paul had ever seen. The three struck up a conversation and he invited them into the wheelhouse. As they stepped in, they became overwhelmed with the aroma of old tobacco and burnt coffee, yet it seemed pleasant, as if it paired well with the smells of the river.

"So, where are you young men going?

"We are going to Paris?" Paul said.

"Ah yes, perhaps to meet a young lady?"

"No", Jean said. "We are going to the university in Metz, we are going to be surgeons. We are just visiting some places that we have never seen before."

"Very good," said the captain. "That is a much needed as well as noble profession."

Their conversation lasted well into the night as they steamed their way up the Marne.

"How often do you stay on the river," Jean asked.

"All the time. I will never leave my love. I had a wife at one time, she was the only one ever meant for me. She died from the pox back in 1848. Ever since then there has been no reason for me to go home. I have been working on this river ever since. This is now my home. It is where I feel her."

It seemed to Jean and Paul to be one of the saddest, yet bravest things they had ever heard. They had never felt that way about anyone, save each other, so it was a little difficult for them to comprehend, but it was not hard to imagine such a love. The captain spoke of it as if it were just matter of fact, not wasted yearning. They stayed in the wheelhouse talking with the captain all night, until they disembarked at Chalon. They headed straight to Chalon's cathedral. There they prayed, thanking God for a safe trip and the opportunity to meet such a noble gentleman as the riverboat captain. Neither of them had ever met anyone that taught them so much in so short a time. They asked God to look over their families and friends, then they thanked Him for the love that he has shown to mankind. They stayed for the night at the Hotel-de-Ville. Other than visiting the cathedrals and the beautiful gardens there was not much to do in Chalon, except drink the regions champagne, which they had never developed a taste for. They only had one day there, so they went to the theatre and attended a show. It was not a fantastically good show, but it was something to do on their night in Chalon. Paul kept thinking about the river boat captain, his love for only one woman, his loss of her, yet his bravery to carry on. Jean did not think too much about it. He focused more on his goals than on other people's misery, but he did have a deep kind of respect for the captain.

The following morning the boat left for Paris. It headed back up the Marne for the last leg of the journey. Jean slept for most of the ride, they were both deprived of sleep and they wanted to be at their best when they arrived in Paris, but Paul was too wound up to sleep. He spent most of the night in the wheelhouse with the captain, he enjoyed the company. They had little conversation, yet Paul was enthralled with this man. He was just a poor boat captain, but one of the richest men Paul had ever met. His wealth was in his heart, it could never be taken from him. The passengers disembarked one by one. Every person heading off to their respective lives, none giving any thought to the other. Paul and Jean gave the captain a fond farewell.

"We will meet again," the captain said as he took off his hat and gave the two a short bow. They left his presence with the hope that if they did meet again, they would find him well. They found lodging at a boarding house that sat directly above a cabaret. It made it hard to sleep at night, but it created many fantastic visions.

They visited the library, it was one of the largest collections of manuscript that either of them had seen, but it was rivaled by the one in Metz. They were proud of the choices that they had made. They visited the theater and watched a show. Neither of these boys ever thought that they would see Paris, they never thought about going. They did love its rich history, its beautiful gardens, and the introduction of women, the sort that they had never seen before. The city, at night, was something from a dream. The lights lit up the night sky. During the day, it was crowded with people, the largest collection of humanity, and inhumanity, either of them had ever seen in one place. It was a life that was far too big for these young boys from a small town. There were people dressed in all kinds of colorful garb. Yellow dresses, blue and orange ones. They all had bustles on that made it look as if the women were hiding a hot air balloon under their backsides. Women in Briey did not dress so elegant, they were more down to Earth, working class folks. These were the people that they missed the most, these folks were their people. They could not, in their hearts, leave their beloved Briey. However, they were here for a new experience. They walked over to the west bank of the Seine, sat with a bottle of wine and looked at the moon. Occasionally elliptical clouds would gently blow past the light side of the moon. Sometimes they blew by so thin that it made the moon look as if it was still an idea that had not quite been born yet. Undoubtedly it was a strange and beautiful night.

"We made it to Paris." Jean said.

"It seems hard to believe that you and I would be

sitting on the bank of the Seine, yet here we are." Paul responded. "

"Yes, here we are." They both felt it, though neither of them said it, but they were sick for home. They covered it up by feigning excitement about being in Paris.

After seeing all the sites that Paris had to offer, and there were many, they made their way south to Chartres. This was a big town, but not like Paris. Paris could swallow you whole and spit out a wrecked resemblance of a man. Chartres was more the type of town that would lick you all over and leave you feeling good about your day. They decided to stay for a few days, this was more their pace. They came from Briey, so medieval sights did not make much of an impression on these two, but the charms of sweet young women did. They were not to be blamed for this, for there was no shortage of said beauties. They went out on the town their second night there. It was a new experience for the two boys. Wine flowed unrestricted, scantily clad women of all classes crowded the street. They went from café to theater to café, it was a night unlike any they had ever had. There was a smell of foreign jasmine that permeated the air, fused with the fragrance of Chinese opium, the sound of gypsy mandolins and tambourines filled the air, their senses going wild, they found their way to the shore of the river Eure, there they talked about their home, which brought them great comfort. They spent some of the best parts of their childhood along the motherly banks of the river that was the vein that ran through their beloved Briey. They felt too grown up for that now, but that did nothing to stop the thought from bringing peace to their young minds. It was their familiarity. Having been out for the past few nights, the pair decided to visit the Chartres Cathedral. They always had the idea of being close to God, in their hearts, they loved Him. Being in the cities that they had grown up hearing legends about now seemed so irrelevant. The history had little to do with advances in science and medicine, so they visited the museums, shrines of science. They stayed for over a week, studying, enjoying the night life, reveling in the fact that they were now well travelled. They attended a cabaret, which they had never done before that night. It turned out to be everything that they had expected it not to be. They had never seen women dressed like that, kicking their legs so high into the air that they were morally inclined to look away every time they kicked. In their minds it was just something that they could say they did, but not with pride. The train for Orleans was to leave the following afternoon and they had every intention of being on it. They made it off the train to the sound of the trains steam whistles. They were deafening, maintaining the same note throughout, it was like a single note symphony. They grabbed their bags and found their way to a hotel, they checked in for the night and went straight to sleep. They had plenty of time to enjoy themselves, but for now, sweet slumber awaited. They dreamed of their homes and the good that they could do back there. There was never any intention in either of their minds to leave Briey permanently, or for too long. The following morning, after a breakfast of cheese filled croissant and coffee, they went to the bank of the river Loire. They sat for many hours watching the people pass by. They were both very anxious to start their university training. This was to be their last stop before they had to be in Metz. They visited the museum at Orleans, it was one of the more fascinating ones they had seen. There were exhibits of medicine from ancient Egypt all the way through to the present. The science exhibits contained one of the most powerful telescopes in the world and displays on the usage of batteries, a source of stored electricity. They spent the day there and considered it to be one of the best days they had had, so far. This was more their pace, they had grown up with a love of learning. Now these two were driving themselves forward with what was best called an unknown, or unrealized ambition, but not in the sense of self-aggrandizement, but in a far more selfless sense. They were changing into fine young men, each with their own personalities. The changes were subtle, but they could both feel them coming on. Paul was always the more jovial sort, the older he got the more that was brought to the forefront of his personality. He did not walk around laughing all day, but he was always up for it. Sometimes he would find humor in a situation that did not call for any. It made sense, he could be reminded of a funny situation in the middle of a situation that was not funny at all. It all just made him a very good-natured person, generous, and concerned for his fellow man. He was an easy person to love, he also loved easily. Some of the simplest things he had ever experienced stuck out in his mind as moments of love. As he got older, he was turning into a very handsome man. His personality just made his physical appearance all the sharper, none of which was realized by Paul himself. In his mind there was only his friendship with Jean and his future as a surgeon. He thought of the river boat captain and the love that he felt for one woman only. He could see himself eventually falling in love with a woman that made up his world, he just hoped that when the time came, if it came, it would be the right one. Jean was a bit more serious, but not unpleasantly so. He loved a good time too. Other things were starting to come into his mind. Namely, the opposite sex. He could feel the attraction, although he was not sure how to handle it. His mind was still set on school, learning to become a surgeon, but now he was starting to think that there were many facets to life, and he wanted to experience them all. He was not sure how to go about it, youth and inexperience seemed to get in the way and the concept of true love never really played a part, but not to his detriment. His idea of true love was his addiction to the desire of practicing medicine, everything else was a distraction. Jean and Paul had decided to treat themselves to a cabaret, helping themselves to overcome a religious fear of immorality. None of their boyhood stories could have prepared them for what they saw that night. Music and dancing, and women, who's dress left nothing to the imagination. The small town of Briey was close knit, here, nobody knew anybody, which enabled a certain freedom of movement, along with many other freedoms. Freedoms that Jean and Paul never confronted before. While at the cabaret, they were approached by a small group of women. Not cabaret girls, just young women, out enjoying themselves. They sat and talked well into the night. The girls were thoroughly impressed with the fact that Jean and Paul were going to be doctors.

These girls had plans of their own too. Jean and Paul were excited to find out what they were. They had spent so much time thinking about themselves and their own careers, a new perspective may be just what they needed. They made plans to meet back there the following evening. The next day was a damp and somewhat dreary day, the evening was a misty one, they could feel the moisture gathering on their clothes, and in their hair. Despite this uncomfortableness they were still very eager with anticipation, they wore it like a dark cloak. They made their way to the cabaret as fast as they could, to avoid any unnecessary moisture from collecting on them. Only two of the girls showed up, they were already there waiting.

"Good evening," Paul said.

"Hello," they replied.

"Only two of you?" Jean asked.

"Yes. I am Michelle, and this is Claudia. We had discussed it amongst ourselves last night, we knew that we couldn't all come, so, Claudia and I won, or lost, that remains to be seen."

They loved this girl's wit. Smart, and beautiful.

"Hopefully, you ladies will not be disappointed," Jean said.

"Hopefully," the two girls nodded in agreement.

The night was still young, the air was rich and vibrant. They had a few glasses of wine at the cabaret, then decided to go to the theater. They were all well entertained. They stayed well into the night on a bench, along the shore of the Loire. Jean and Paul had never had anyone to talk with, save each other. There was a certain freedom in talking with someone that you do not know very well. Jean told the two girls how much the river had always meant to them. It was like a dark flowing blanket that kept those warm that loved it. They enjoyed the company of these two young ladies. They had come from good families, and they had been well educated. Claudia was very much interested in science and medicine, Michelle was more interested in art and theater. It gave them a lot to talk about. They enjoyed this interaction enough to stay for another week. That still left them a week to get to Metz and get ahead on their studies. They knew that they would be up against some of the most studious minds in Europe, and they had no intention of falling behind. They viewed this new company as a pleasant distraction, unsure if they wanted it to be more than that or not. They visited each other often, the girls coming to their room every day. They took long walks by the shore, through the old town, and visited many sights to occupy their time and give themselves an excuse to spend time together. On one afternoon Paul walked into the room and found Jean and Claudia kissing and touching each other in places that Paul never would have thought about touching. He turned and walked away because he had no idea what to make of that situation. He never said a word to anyone about that, he would not have known what to say anyhow. The following day as the four of them walked along the river's edge Jean and Claudia were holding hands, it made Paul a bit uncomfortable. Michelle turned and looked at Paul, she caught him looking at her. Perceiving Paul's nervousness, she took his hand in hers, he smiled at her, and suddenly felt his uneasiness melt away. They all walked around until late in the evening, no one wanting to let go of the others hand. Paul was not sure if it was love, but he was sure that it was the closest he had ever come to it. Claudia recommended a play for the following evening, "Le Tartuffe." Although Jean and Paul were well-educated, they were not overly indulged in culture. This was a relatively new experience for them, one that they could get used to, if it did not threaten their singularity, or their simplicity. It was not as much seeing nice plays, going to theaters, dances, it was going to these events with new people. In the past Jean and Paul only had each other, now they had two new companions to go with, to talk with, although they still depended on each other more than anyone else. There was little to no evidence that would ever change. Jean and Paul had depended on each other too much, for too long. Feelings among these four were growing like the shadow of a giant pine as it gets later in the day. The days before Jean and Paul had to be in Metz were winding down. One more day and one more night, then they would be off. Paul felt the need to talk with Michelle about his feelings for her.

"Why?" Jean asked.

"Because I owe her at least that."

"You do not owe her anything."

Paul thought about that for a while. Maybe he did not owe her an explanation, but he did owe himself one. Michelle was such a kind person, Paul did not wish to leave Orleans with any heartache, nor did he plan to leave any behind. Paul and Jean were both gentle souls, but Paul was a bit more sensitive. When Paul met up with

Michelle that evening, he told her, sadly, that they would be leaving for Metz the following afternoon.

"I know." Michelle said with a tear welling up in her left eye. He could tell that she was holding back many more, as was he.

"I promise that I will write to you." Michelle said.

"I will write to you too, as often as I can."

Jean and Claudia's evening went much different. They had been intimate the night before they were to leave. The goodbyes at the train station the following afternoon were a bit awkward. Due to the carnal knowledge shared between Jean and Claudia, they said goodbye like perfect strangers. Paul and Michelle's separation went more like that of lovers, sharing tears as the train beckoned them for a certain unknown chasm. They boarded the train as it groaned like a giant waking up unwillingly. A roar erupted from deep in its throat, its bones creaked. They were wondering how this old piece of machinery could still move. After a few heaves it was off with more force than either of them imagined.

"What's that all about?" Jean asked just as the train was getting underway.

"I don't know what you mean."

"That goodbye," Jean said. "You two were crying."

"I'm going to miss her. I love her."

"Paul," Jean said. "I had sex with Claudia and I'm not going to miss her."

"Sex and love are not the same thing my friend. Can we really be sold so cheap?"

"I suppose you are right Paul." Jean replied as they settled in for the journey.

-4-

It was an eight-hour train ride to Metz, considering the stopovers. There was a heated anticipation between the two of them, setting off to do what they had wanted to do all their lives. Every step closer to their goal brought renewed excitement. That is all that Jean could think about, Paul thought about that too, and he thought of Michelle. It was an odd feeling for him, to think of someone in this way, he could not have stopped if he wanted to. The train was filled with an assortment of characters. All colors and manners of dress. There were balloon dresses, as Jean and Paul had come to call them. Dresses without corsets but hemmed up enough that they did not drag on the ground. The train was filled with vibrant colors, more so than the circus. There was a beautiful blue dress wrapped around the last person that they wanted to see it on. She was trying to strike up a conversation with a stately looking gentleman that looked to be twice her age. A handsome man that appeared to be as disinterested as everyone else. The porter was walking by with a tray full of drinks, even he was disinterested in her attempts at conversation. Eventually she stopped talking and gave up on any further attempts at conversation with strangers, so she talked with herself in a low voice. In the back of the car there sat a gorgeous red headed woman with a dress the color of a spring field. She caught the eye of everyone in the car. She was half-heartedly involved in a conversation with a German gentleman. It was as obvious that she did not want to be rude any more than she wanted to be in this conversation.

Her eyes looked far away as if she was dreaming of someplace else, someplace as beautiful as she was. None the less, there she was, stuck. Jean and Paul knew that the only satisfying conversation that they could have would be with each other. Everyone else was just a pair of eyes. The train had stopped, some of the people got off, only to be replaced with new creatures. The two were eagerly awaiting their arrival in Metz. They still had hours to go so they entertained themselves in other ways. As people moved their lips in conversation they would fill in with imaginary sentences. Finally, after they became bored with that, they started to discuss medical procedures. Thinking about new and innovative methods of performing surgeries. They were only ideas, but it kept their conversation going. The rhythm of the steel wheels beneath their feet was like a narcotic, before too long they were both fast asleep. They awoke about an hour outside of Metz. They resumed their conversation about the medical field as if it had never stopped. The two boys discussed medicine, and what their area of expertise might be. They both wanted to be the most sought after in the medical field.

Arriving in Metz, they stepped off the train feeling as if this was there town, believing they belonged there. They went to the school administration and were assigned a dorm room. By request the two of them were assigned to the same room. It could not be imagined that they would be in separate rooms, not these two. There were three days until their studies would commence. Choosing to use this time to their own advantage, they studied at the library and at the museum, they even visited the city morgue. If they could not tolerate being around a dead body, they would never make it as surgeons. In June of 1868 classes began. The surgery room was a very spartan affair, with four stone slabs, but it was well lit by a giant window in the roof and mirrors spread throughout the room. It was an ancient way of lighting a room, but it worked remarkably well. The walls were very sparse, no pictures of great masters of the medical field, just a few torches spread throughout the room. Everyone was given a cadaver to dissect and identify the internal organs. Within the first week of training twelve students left. Some vomited, some even cried. The idea that that body was someone, a son, a brother, a sister, it was all too much for some to handle. It was obvious that surgery was not for them. Jean and Paul progressed wonderfully; it was obvious that this was where they belonged. They absorbed knowledge of the human anatomy at an alarming pace. All their free time they spent either at the library, studying in their dorm, or at the museum where they could see all the advances in medicine that had been made over the centuries. The two progressed to the point of not only identifying trauma to specific organs, but also the cause. They could identify heart congestion, severed arteries, kidney failure, and cirrhosis of the liver, among many other causes of sickness and death. The two of them would still do mock surgeries on each other in their spare time. They loved the work they were doing, and the idea of saving lives thrilled them. Their instructors, great, and experienced surgeons themselves, were impressed, they expected to see great things from Jean and Paul. In the summer of

1869, the two went home to Briey to visit with old friends and family. Their families were still close, even in their absence. One could see the pride beaming from the faces of their families, especially their fathers. Average foundry workers whose sons were to be surgeons. They imagined the pride that the entire village would feel, two of their own becoming important people. One of the proudest of them was the old baker. He came to see them upon hearing of their return. He brought them pastries and sweets as he did when they were children. In his eyes they were children, the only ones that he had ever claimed as his own. Before they were to return to Metz, they went into the field for a picnic, just as they used to do when they were just boys. The smell of lavender was thick in the air. The field of beautiful, purple flowers was the perfect place, Eden. The Meuse flowed beside the edge of the field, then disappeared into a distant meadow. The beauty of their village and the surrounding farms always stayed with them. They fished in the Meuse and gave their catch to the old baker. They had not fished in what seemed like a long time. It reminded them of their childhood, which was an incredibly happy time. They eagerly awaited the finishing of their classes so they could return to Briey and practice their profession.

Upon their return to the university classes resumed. Now they were studying brain trauma. There was a total of three cadavers for all fourteen students. The cadavers were all male, two appeared to be in their mid to late twenties, whereas the third looked like he was in his fifties. They could not be viewed as humans because the student's emotions could get the better of them. They had to be viewed as learning tools. Everyone was divided into teams of five, except Jean's team, it consisted of only four students. Two of the cadavers had died from head injuries, the third was to be a simulation, the creation of, and repair of a head injury. In sight of the class the instructor clubbed the third cadaver, caving in the back of its skull. Much of the class turned away at the sound of the skull cracking, Jean and Paul were not among them. Each team had to quickly analyze the extent of the trauma, if the patient could be saved, then, what would be necessary to save said patient, and do it. Paul and Jean were on different teams, much to their disapproval. It turned out beneficial, the two teams would not have passed if not for Jean and Paul, the third team failed. As it turned out, neither Jean, nor Paul's patient could have been saved. They included this analysis in their dissertations, but they went through the motions of saving their patients anyway. Based on Paul's examination, swelling of the brain was inevitable. Tiny holes were punched into the skull and the blood and fluid was suctioned out. A metal plate was used to patch the hole in the cadaver's skull. Jean's patient was killed by a bullet through the forehead. There was no exit wound, but there was a small crack in the back of the skull. After cutting and peeling away that part of the scalp, a cut was made to remove that portion of the skull. The bullet was then removed, and a small metal plate was screwed into place to patch that part of the skull. The same was done for the forehead. Upon finishing this procedure, the scalp was then stitched back into place. The two teams passed with honors. The procedures of all three teams was done under the scrutiny of the instructors. They were most impressed with the forward and advanced thinking of Jean and Paul, both of whom were at the helm of their respective teams. They were learning a lot and they were learning it fast. It surprised everyone, their instructors, families, even themselves. Growing up they knew what they wanted to do, but they did not know that it would be so easy for them, almost natural.

Paul had received a letter from Michelle. He was so excited he could not wait to read it to Jean. She had started learning art and theater in Paris. She was happy with her studies, but she missed Paul tremendously and hoped that they could be together after school was over.

"I guess that is love." Jean said.

Receiving and replying to letters from home, and from Michelle had become a regular part of their weekly routine. Their parents would often write to tell them how proud they were of them. They would pass along greetings and well wishes from the village, especially the old baker, who had enjoyed their company for so many years. He often spoke with their parents, discovering how well the boys were doing, and reminiscing about the two boy's childhood. He loved and missed them dearly.

Training at the university was still as exciting as the first day, now it had become rewarding as well. They had recently learned about blood flow, the closing of severed arteries, and many other things regarding the circulatory system. This time in their life seemed to be the best, with the expectation that the future held out the promise of even better times. In the winter of 1870 Jean and Paul took the train to Paris, they wanted to visit with

Claudia and Michelle. They had taken three days from University to see the only friends that they really had. There were people that they loved at home in Briey. Of course, their families, friends from secondary school, and the old baker that had always been so kind to them. They often mentioned him in their letters back home.

Paris was just as they remembered it. It was the same as it was when they had tried to forget it. Dirty, crowded, and without much care for humanity. The only difference now was that two people that they cared very much for lived there. Michelle and Claudia met them at the train station. It was a warm and happy reunion. They went to a play at the school that Michelle was in, she was incredibly good, and when it was over the crowd stood up applauding. Michelle did not expect a standing ovation, it made her cry. They all hugged and told her what a remarkable job she did, she really was incredible. In Paul's eyes she was nothing short of angelic. After the performance, the four of them went out for some wine and everyone talked about how well things were going for them. Claudia was studying microbiology under the tutelage of Louis Pasteur. She was doing very well in her studies for the cure of infectious diseases. Jean and Paul were especially interested since they were in the medical field. They talked well into the night each one overly impressed with the other, and all feeling a bit self-satisfied. The following day they sat on the bank of the Seine. Rivers had always put Jean and Paul at ease, they were very peaceful and reminded them of all that was good in the world. Paul and Michelle were happy to be spending time together. They made plans without really knowing whether they could make them come true. Jean and Claudia ran off to God knows where, but Paul had a fairly good idea what for. It really did not matter to him, he was enjoying his private time with Michelle, what a beautiful creature she was, inside and out. He was overwhelmed with a sudden desire to finish school so the two of them could be together, she felt the same. He told her all about life in Briey and Metz. He promised to go wherever she wanted. When the time came to say goodbye, they all took a carriage to the station. Paul and Michelle gave each other a small kiss that held the promise of better things in the future. Claudia and Jean just said goodbye as if they were mad at each other. Jean and Paul returned to the university and resumed their studies. The next phase of their education was to diagnose and treat living patients. This made everyone nervous, it was one thing to work on the dead, but working on the living could cost them their life. To take every precaution the instructors would be taking the first several cases with the students working as assistants. The first few were common cases of flu, fever, or just a cold, they even had a couple of cases of broken legs and arms. They learned quite a lot about setting broken limbs. These two were turning out to be fine doctors. The instructors were quite impressed with Jean and Paul's willingness to take on any case. They went back and forth from the university to the hospital where they were interning. They had delivered babies, set broken bones, and assisted with several surgeries of all different sorts. They were advanced enough and very diligent with their work that they would be graduating within the year. Paul wrote a letter to Michelle that said, "My dearest Michelle, the memories of when I last saw you have stayed on my mind. I cannot nor will not forget you. I am finishing my university training this fall, at that point I will come to you. Please, do not forget me, or the promises that I made to you. Yours forever."

When Michelle read the letter, she became overcome with anticipation. Her love would be coming to her. She felt like a princess whose dreams will all come true. She was still studying the theatrical arts, but, for now, all she could think of was Paul. Maybe he could start his own practice in Paris, or maybe they will go somewhere that they have never been. She decided that she would follow Paul anywhere, a decision that Paul had made a long time ago.

A letter had arrived from home for Paul and Jean. Their parents had heard disturbing rumors abounding that spring of 1870 about a unification of Prussia and the southern German states. That information did not affect the university students. It seemed to make France very uneasy, but classes continued without any regard for the politics of the day. Throughout their time at university they would go to St. Stephens to pray. They had much to be grateful for. The figures in the stained glass seemed to speak to them. The image of the Virgin had a calming effect. It was almost as if their mothers were in Metz with them, letting them know that they were going to be all right. The image of God, the all-powerful creator, provided them with a feeling of protective power, as if no weapon formed against them would find success.

-5-

On July 16th of that year France declared war on Prussia. It became official on July 19th when French forces invaded Prussian territory. The French marched within miles of Metz to occupy the German town of Saarbrucken. Drums and bugles could faintly be heard. Within four days of the French occupation the first battle of the war broke out when the Prussian forces overran the French garrison at Wissembourg. The French forces, greatly outnumbered, fought bravely and brought no discredit to the first corp. All of this was less than fifty miles from Metz. The artillery fire could be heard in Metz. It sounded like thunder that would light up the sky. The students at the university could not even imagine the scale of the slaughter that was taking place. War was unlike anything that an education in advanced medicine could prepare them for. There was a great fortress within the city walls of Metz, it was foolish to think that it would escape the war untouched, yet the majority went through their day thinking just that. Jean and Paul's hearts were breaking over the possibility of what may happen to their beloved Metz, more importantly, their beloved Briey. Within days the Prussian army defeated the French at the battle of Spicheren, driving them from Saarbrucken. Jean and Paul could only imagine the cost of human life and the suffering endured by the uninvolved innocent.

The following day the Dean of the university announced that classes were to be put on hold, pending the outcome of the war. This was a devastating blow to Jean and Paul, their futures hinged on their completing their training at the university. They did not understand why their education should be put off because of a war that they had no interest in. Most of the students stayed on in Metz, hoping for a quick French victory. Jean and Paul decided to put their knowledge and skill to practical use. They decided to follow the army and help with the wounded wherever and whenever they could. After all, this is what they were trained for, and it was where they knew they could do the most good. They had no idea what that would entail, a decision that could be questioned forever. The battle of Wissembourg was over, there was nothing they could do to help there. War was foreign to them, apart from stories they heard while growing up. They had learned of various wars when they were in history class during their tenure in secondary school, but they learned quickly that books, and real-life experience were not even comparatively close to the same thing. They feared what may lay ahead, not for themselves, but for the innocent. They had moments of excitement when they would imagine all the people that would be saved by their very own hands, but it never lasted. There were never any illusions of grandeur amongst them, only pity for those that they knew with all their heart to be suffering. Paul had got a letter off to Michelle just before they left Metz. He prayed for her well-being, and he let her know how much she meant to him. He dreamed of her a thousand times a day. He could not help himself; he was in love. He thought of her in the theater that fateful night, and when she saw his unease and took his hand while walking along the bank of the Seine. That was the moment that he knew he loved her. Paul hoped with all his heart that the horrors of war would not touch her, nor come anywhere near her, his beloved Michelle.

Two days later was the battle of Worth. As they approached the field of battle, they could hear what sounded like the incessant humming of the wings of a million butterflies. As they got closer, they realized it was the groaning of thousands of dying men. There was blood and body parts everywhere. No amount of education could ever had prepared them for this. Immediately, with the courage that they provided for each other, they began to work. The first soldier they approached was bleeding profusely from a wound in his leg, he had lost a lot of blood. Jean began to cauterize the wound to prevent any further blood loss. Throughout this procedure the soldier cried, begging to be allowed to see his mother one last time. This was a deal that he must have been making with his creator, what he was asking for was totally out of the hands of Jean and Paul. Being devout men themselves they could understand his pleading. They cauterized the wound in the Frenchman's leg, wrapped it up with an antibiotic ointment and told him that he would be fine, unsure themselves whether, or not, that would be the case. They were able to find the living because of the moaning and the pleas for help. The dead made no noise at all, yet they touched these two the deepest. They worked their way through the battlefield helping French and Prussian alike. The cries were the same, last ditch efforts to make a deal with God. This was the saddest moment of their lives. This from two young men that had never experienced sadness, at least not in a permanent form, not the kind that stays with you throughout your years. There is a sadness that lies hidden in the hearts of man, silently waiting for the opportunity to reveal itself in the most hideous way possible. Once revealed it never truly leaves, it just waits for the moments that it can wake one from sleep. They worked their way through the field, saving all that they could. Many died in their arms with requests like "tell my family that I love them". Requests that were impossible for Paul and Jean to carry out, yet they promised to do whatever they could, just to give some comfort to the dying, then they would pray with them. If they could not save them in this life, they begged God to forgive them and to take these soldiers into His embrace, where they may find joy forever. As they worked their way across the field of battle, they approached the Prussian side with some reservations. It was mutually decided that it was their job to heal, to save lives, regardless of nationality. They found that the Prussian boys were just like the French. No one wanted to die in this killing field all alone, with only Jean and Paul to comfort them. Many did receive comfort because of these two, but for most, comfort was all that Jean and Paul could provide. They worked long and hard to save these poor souls that had been wrecked by this war, and they knew that it would continue. They prayed that it would end, but it did not, the fighting continued, and Jean and Paul were left wondering why. They rested for the night underneath a pine grove, far away from the field that had left them bloody in body, and spirit. They had a troubled sleep that night. All through the night they could hear the cawing of crows that were either at Worth, or on their way there. It was a free feast for every sort of ravenous animal, winged and four legged alike. It amazed them, how little some men thought of the lives of other men, blindly feeding them to the war machine. The Prussian army went on the march northwest towards Metz. For a week they marched, for a week Jean and Paul followed them from a safe distance. Along the road lay the dead and dying soldiers, French and Prussian alike. The last casualties from the battle of Worth. Jean and Paul carried no tools to bury any of the dead, but they had medical supplies to help the wounded. Many died, bled out while the two were trying to staunch the flow of blood. They would look at each other, shake their heads, say a prayer for the dead, and then continue up the road. Sometimes they would walk for hours without seeing anyone, living or dead. Just as their hopes would rise, they would come across others, victims of a nation's quest for power. Jean thought to himself how the quest for power made people so irrelevant. They felt irrelevant too, especially when a young man, about their age died under their hands. His name was Luc, from Marsal. He was along the road, gravely injured from a bullet that had went into his abdomen and exited the left side of his upper back.

"Am I going to live?" Luc asked, while they tried to give him as much medical attention as they could while on the side of a muddy road.

"Of course, you will!" Paul exclaimed. "You are going to live forever."

"Thank you." Luc said.

Jean looked over Luc at Paul and sadly shook his head. There was far too much damage to save him.

"Luc, tell us about Marsal."

"Oh," he said, after coughing up blood, which Paul

immediately wiped away so that Luc would not see it. It is a beautiful little town, not even twenty miles from here, you will see when we get there."

"Yes," Jean replied, "I believe it will be beautiful."

"It is, there is a field of lavender south and east of the town. I always run through the fields with my brother and sister. Sometimes we would lay down and watch the butterflies fly over us and pretend that they are angels, it was like being in heaven."

"We are from Briey, we too have a field of lavender around our village," Paul said, as a lone tear ran down his face. Jean noticed that Luc had passed, but he could not stop Paul, he had to hear this as well. Tears began to flow down Jean's face as Paul went on. "We have green dairy pasturage to the north, the finest dairy in all of France." It was unclear if Paul was still speaking with Luc, or for his own benefit. "We are only a short ride from Metz, where Jean and I study medicine. I have a love in Paris that I will marry after this war ends. Jean, we have to take Luc home."

"I know." Jean replied.

The two of them made a stretcher and carried Luc to Marsal, passing bodies on the road as they labored on. As they approached from the southeast, they saw that it was just as Luc had described, beautiful. This field made their hearts cry out for home, but they knew that they could not return, not yet. Coming into the town square, it was a short time before they were surrounded by the villagers, murmurs of "Luc" were heard throughout the crowd. They heard a small boy raising his voice in the crowd, "Luc, Luc," a boy of about twelve came running up to them "my brother, my brother, this is my brother."

"Where do you live boy?" Jean asked.

"Follow me," the boy said through a tear and dirt smeared face. When they arrived, the boy ran into his house. Before Jean and Paul could reach the door, the boy's father came outside.

"My son, Luc, what happened to my son? My boy, how much I love you. You have always made your family proud. May you be with God."

"Your son, Luc, was a fine man. He told us about his family and his home before he passed."

"You two were with him at the end?"

"Yes sir. We are doctors trying to care for the injured of this war. We found your boy along the roadside, we did all that we could."

"For that we are grateful. We will bury him tomorrow, you must stay." "Thank you, sir, but we are following the army and we must continue," Jean said.

"Surely you are tired and hungry. You must stay. At the end you two were the only friends that my Luc had."

It had been a long time since they slept under a proper roof, or even had a proper meal. They were convinced to stay. Luc's family fed them and put them up for the night. The two of them lay side by side in Luc's old bedroom.

"Do you think we are doing the right thing?" Paul asked.

"What do you mean?"

"Following the army around, I mean, maybe we should be going home."

"This is what we pledged to do, you and me. How could we go home now, with thousands in need of our care?"

"You are right. I did not mean to bring it up, it was just a thought. Goodnight." Paul said.

The following morning the two of them awoke to the sound and smell of breakfast being prepared. They had slept a lot longer than usual, they had become accustomed to little sleep. Jean and Paul got up and greeted the family. They had breakfast then headed to the square for Luc's funeral. It seemed as if the entire town had come out, the square was filled. A priest led the procession to the cemetery, followed by the casket, then Luc's family, who had asked Jean and Paul to walk with them. Everyone wept, Luc was very well loved. Paul silently wondered how their village would feel if something happened to them. After the funeral, a short goodbye, and heartfelt thanks for the sustenance and rest, the two got back on the road towards Metz.

Once they had gotten back on the path of the dead, there was no more dying, and the dead became fewer and farther between. It was not difficult to follow the path that had been taken by the army, everything was in a state of disarray. A giant swath of land had been torn up. Heading straight for Metz fleeing civilians told them that the army was at Vionville east of Mars-La-Tour. Since the Prussians were on the offensive it made more sense to follow them from a safe distance, and then come in afterwards and try to clean up the mess. Mars-La-Tour was less than twenty miles from their village, they were very fearful that Briey may not be spared the atrocities of war. As they continued tending to the wounded a Prussian officer that had been shot through the hand informed them that on that very day the city of Metz had come under siege. He thanked them for their care of the men on both sides of the battle, he said that he did not know if anyone else would have done that. Their thoughts went immediately to Metz, their fellow students, their instructors, and St. Stephens cathedral, the place that they had always sought solace in the hand of God. It seemed that God had abandoned these fields of blood a long time ago. Perhaps God was growing weary over these petty squabbles among men that only lead to death. Profaning God with their arrogance.

In the field of Mars-La-Tour it was evident that the Prussians had mastered the use of artillery. There were relatively few victims of gunshot wounds, but thousands that had been blown apart by the explosive shells from artillery batteries. Many were bleeding profusely from parts of their bodies that had been blown off. They staunched the flow of blood as best as they could, but inside the two of them were beginning to feel helpless. They thought often about their families and how they might be doing in the darkness of this war. They missed them very much and often talked about it with each other. They imagined themselves laying on that bloody field, unsure of what had happened to them, crying out in pain for those that they loved. They considered leaving the battlefields behind and going home, or even going to Paris to visit with Claudia and Michelle. It was strange, the things that war, or even the sight of war did to people, not just the combatants, but their families and friends. These were normal, hard-working folks, that would be changed forever. In the end they decided that healing people was their calling and they would just have to look past the ghastly scenes that entailed. There was much crying and torment on the field, blue skies above, a beautiful scene, below it was pure hell. More of their patients died than survived, that could not be helped. Poorly equipped and performing surgery in fields of mud and blood. Everyone was susceptible to infections and diseases. Of the hundreds upon hundreds that were wounded about six men were able to be saved, this was disheartening. The armies had moved away heading northeast, leaving their dead and dying to rot in the summer sun. This was inhumane beyond their comprehension. They began to fear deeply for their families, the armies were heading towards Briey. They were stopped by the French at Gravelotte. This turned out to be one of the bloodiest battles of the war. From the explosion of the first volley of artillery, which blew a gaping hole in the French front line, to the repulse of the Prussian infantry that tried to pour through it. This horrid scene left them with much work to do. They had never considered being workers like their fathers, it was not meant to be. They had chosen their professions from a young age. Their intent had always been to help people. They were beginning to see the downside of that commitment. Their minds told them that they were doing the right thing, but their hearts were being slowly ripped apart. The gravity of how close to home this hit was unthinkable. They were in constant fear for their village and those within. At Gravelotte, while tending to the wounded, they came across a young girl. She had followed her father from Charleville, he was in the army. She was hugging his dead body, what was left of it. She was injured from shrapnel in her shoulder. She did not even notice her own injury, she just cried for her father, begging him to come back to her. Jean and Paul cried with her, the final realization of what war did to people hit them, not necessarily the dead, but the survivors, and yet, still they pressed on. They stayed there with that poor girl until they patched her up and convinced her to go back home. There was absolutely nothing left for her there. They walked with her off the battlefield in the direction of Charleville and just let her keep walking. The two of them had much work to do. This was the largest and bloodiest battle they had ever seen. The extreme level of carnage would have made weaker men lose any, and all faith in humanity. Fortunately, Jean and Paul were not weaker men, but they were still men. In this life, their profession, they showed unlimited determination in pursuit of their goals, but they were becoming troubled. The battle of Gravelotte was unlike anything that they had ever seen. Once seen it cannot be unseen, this was the start of their personal troubles. Some things are just harder to get past than others, this was one of them. They debated on going back to Metz but decided against it due to the city being under siege. Instead they followed the French army to Sedan, stopping back home in Briey along the way. Everyone was so glad to see them. There was excitement throughout the village at the return of these two native sons. They wanted to get caught up and say hi to everyone, knowing that they would be leaving in a couple of days. Jean and Paul's families got together for dinner that first night of their return. That was when their families broke some bad news to them. Their old secondary school teacher had died two weeks earlier. This was the saddest news that they had received since they had been away. They had loved that woman as if she was their adopted mother. She had loved them as her own prodigy, she encouraged them in their studies and had always seen the potential in these two. After dinner they went to the cemetery to visit with her for what could be the last time, and give her their last words, she deserved that as well as more than they could deliver. Sitting at the graveside they apologized for not being there at the time that she needed them the most. The guilt felt by these two was an intense burning in their hearts. Although they were guilty of nothing, death tends to share its misery by imposing guilt on the innocent. They tried talking each other through the pain. Nothing they could say or do would make the pain go away, save for having each other. Throughout their whole lives they have always been one another's pillar, but even pillars crack under burden after some time. They cried for quite some time thinking about her kindness. That helped as much as putting a bandage on a pillars crack.

"Do you remember when I had a crush on Mrs. Bardin?" Jean asked.

"Yes, I remember."

"She explained to me that she was too old for me and that she loved me in a different kind of way. Until that day I never knew that there was more than one kind of love."

"There always had been, you and I just did not know it." Paul replied.

"I'll miss her just the same."

The following morning, they both awoke in their respective homes, had breakfast, then Jean walked over to Paul's to see if he wanted to go fishing. Still burdened by the self-imposed guilt of their teacher's death, they decided fishing in the river Meuse, which had always been a dear friend to them, was a good idea. They walked through the edge of town to the river. As they walked, they admired at how purple and fragrant the lavender was this time of year. The purple was contrasted with the fluttering of small yellow butterflies, their wings wafting the fragrance higher into the air. All of God's creatures enjoyed this field, it was a place of peace. As they came upon the river, they heard the splash of a couple of turtles that had been sunning themselves on the bank, their approaching spooked them into the water. They started catching fish immediately, some small, some large, but edible all the same. In all, they caught nine fish. Jean had five, and Paul had four. After they stopped fishing, they laid on the bank of the Meuse discussing themselves and their possible fate. They knew that they would be heading back to the battle front soon. The two of them started back for their homes.

"Go ahead Jean, I'm going to stop by Marie's and see if she could use these fish."

"All right, don't do anything that I would not."

"Believe me," Paul said. "I would not do anything that you would do."

Paul traipsed to the west end of the village, he could vividly remember where Marie lived, where he had left the May Day basket those years ago. He knocked, after waiting a moment, she came to the door holding a baby, she held that baby close.

"Oh my god," she said. "I never expected to see you at my door."

"How are you Marie?"

"It's been rough, but we are pulling through it."

"Is that your baby?"

"Yes. He was born two months ago."

"Where is his father?"

Marie started crying and said that he had been killed at the battle of Wissembourg. He was the patriotic sort that believed it was his duty to fight, or die, for France.

"I'm so sorry Marie. I had not heard. I've seen much tragedy in these times, it only seems to get worse."

"Why didn't you love me when we were here growing up?"

"I did not know exactly what that meant." Paul said while being taken aback.

"What about now?" Marie asked.

"Yes. Now I know."

As Paul turned to leave Marie asked, "Was it you that gave me that May Day basket?"

"It was Marie, I'm sorry."

Paul was not sure what he was apologizing for, perhaps his inability to help. His feelings overwhelmed him. Why did Marie's husband have to die, leaving her with an infant? Why did he never love her? Would things have been different if he had never left. Those were the thoughts of guilt rattling around in his head, none of which could ever have been helped. Paul made his way back to his parent's house, trying to wrap his mind around the thousands of tragedies that had been unfolding around him every day. He could see no end to it, only the hope that eventually it would, and he clung to it by a thread.

When he got back home his mother handed him a handful of letters that had come in over the past couple of weeks. They were all from Michelle in Paris. He ran up to his room to read the letters in private. He read them chronologically.

"Dearest Paul.

I think of you every day and most every minute of every day. My fear grows with the passing of time that I cannot hear that you are all right. I know that you are doing what you are meant to do. I, for my part, am meant to love you. School is going well, but I feel empty without you here to share it with, it seems all for naught. Please be safe. Remember I will always love you."

When Paul read these words, he felt his heart rise and fall at the same moment. He knew that he could not just take off for Paris, his only hope was to get through this war alive. He wrote her back saying as much. His heart was with her and had been since the day they met.

They had heard that the French army had taken a northerly route to evade the Prussians, circle around and relieve the city of Metz. Knowing that they had to leave they said a long goodbye to their families. Their fathers took them aside and said to them, "Boys, we know that what you are doing is the right thing, but we also know that it is dangerous. We just want to let you know how much we love you and that you two have made us both proud. Now, please be careful and do not take any unnecessary risks. Promise us that."

"We promise," they both said simultaneously.

That afternoon Jean and Paul struck out on the road in a northeasterly direction hoping to catch up with the army. They picked up on the trail of the army easily enough. It was leading towards Sedan on the Belgian border. The distance was quite far, but they could never miss where an army had been. There is always a swath of disregard and destruction. Half-eaten cattle and sheep littered the sides of the road rotting in the late August weather. The smell was terrible, the odor of war. It would turn the stomach of the highest constitution. Still, the two of them carried on. It was an arduous journey and the cooler fall weather was starting to set in. They were at least a day and a half behind the army. Armies tended to move slowly, so there was little doubt that they would catch up. Everyone was praying for a French victory, no one knew what a Prussian victory might mean for France. Jean and Paul, while aware of the potential outcome, remained concerned with saving lives. They liked being French, maybe even a bit proud of it, but it never overly concerned them. Crossing paths with an old man sitting on the side of the road, they asked if the army had passed and how long ago. "Ah yes," he replied. "They passed this way yesterday evening, but they are held up about a mile east of here at Sedan."

"Will they be moving on?" Jean asked.

"No. Prussians have got them surrounded. Napoleon the Third is with the army. He will most certainly be killed or captured."

"Thank you, sir."

"I do not advise getting any closer, it will certainly be of the utmost danger."

"Perhaps we will just sit with you for a while."

"That would be fine," the old man replied.

That spot on the side of the road felt like purgatory to these two, it was the saddest, loneliest place on Earth.

"Can you hear that?" The old man asked in a sage kind of way.

"Hear what?" Jean asked.

"The country is crying. See how it sags under the weight of its own tears. Where are the birds that sat in the trees and sang to us? Where are the deer that rubbed against them with their gentle caress? Everyone has fled, man and beast. Fled before this invasion of irreverence. Our children are trampled under the boots of indifference."

They did not know if this old man was a poet or simply crazy, they decided that he was indeed a poet, a crazy poet.

"What is it that you do?" Jean asked.

"Whatever I want to, and some things that I do not." That was the old man's reply. It left Jean and Paul confused and wondering.

"Well, what are you doing now?" Paul asked.

"Talking with you and waiting."

"Waiting for what?"

"Waiting for my fate, but I do not think that it will arrive before this war is over. Until then I will sit here and listen to the cannons roaring and I will cry."

Paul and Jean knew exactly what that meant. How many times had they sat on the battlefield and wept, they had seen the result of war first-hand.

A gentle breeze was blowing its cool September breath. Carrying with it the stench of indifference that death holds sway over man.

Tears started to roll down the old man's face with the distant, but distinct crack of the first cannon fire. His lips moved in what appeared to be a silent prayer. The two of them could not help themselves, they prayed too. They prayed for those that had died and for those that were about to. The sound of exploding artillery shells and gunfire filled the distant air. Imagining what was happening, based on prior experiences with the aftermath of battles fought, they too cried. The tears stopped before the battle of Sedan did. The battle raged for about two days, during which time none of them ate or slept. First the sound of gunfire stopped, then the sound of artillery faded as if it were a distant memory. They waited for over twelve hours at the behest of the old man.

"Now, let us all go meet our fate," said the old man.

These words terrified Jean and Paul. They did not believe this to be their fate at all, just their duty.

-6-

As they trudged their way a few miles to the battlefield they came upon a scene of carnage that was beyond anything the two of them expected. Thousands lay dead, blown apart by the impartial judgement of artillery fire. Many lay dying, groaning away their terminal breaths. Tens of thousands were being led away as prisoners of war. Paul and Jean went to work immediately. This war was overwhelming them. They were trained to cure that which could be cured. War was a disease that lay beyond the skill of any doctor, but it still, at least had to be treated. As they removed a bullet from an injured soldier, they saw the old man praying over the dead while Jean and Paul tried to keep the living alive. They realized that under the conditions of a bloody, muddy battlefield, it was hard to save any one's life, they usually only succeeded in prolonging it. Whether their patients lived or not affected them emotionally, but not as much as not holding to their oath would have. While cauterizing the wound of a French soldier that had been shot through the upper thigh, they noticed the old man praying over a dead Prussian. The old man then went rifling through the soldier's pockets and put coins into his own. If Jean and Paul had not been busy carrying on with their duties, and their own feelings, they may have gotten upset. As it were, this was neither the time nor the place for that. The soldier's thigh was bleeding profusely. Paul and Jean had a finger in each hole made by that bullet. They were working with one hand each, and yet it was not clumsy, but precise. Jean would pull his finger from the wound and Paul's finger was already there to replace it.

In this method they saved several lives that day. Where had the old man gone off to? They cauterized hundreds of wounds, a lot of lives were saved, even more were not.

On their eighteenth hour of working they were approached by a Prussian officer that had ten soldiers with him, all at his disposal.

"Was machst du hier?"

"Uh," Paul stammered. "We are doctors, we...

"Auf Deutsch!" The officer demanded.

Neither Jean nor Paul had any more than a basic understanding of German, so they just stood there and looked confused.

"Nehmen Sie sie weg, jetzt."

The soldiers stepped forward and grabbed the two of them and started to lead them away toward a human train of prisoners.

"Wait," Jean said. "Wir sind Arzte."

"Halten." The soldiers stopped as the officer looked them over. "Gehen."

They were immediately arrested for scavenging the battlefield, nothing of which they had ever done, but would now pay for. They were put into a line that stretched as far as the eyes could see, marching northwest towards Belgium. Periodic posts of Prussian soldiers insured that no one would escape. Everyone was so weak, they could not have resisted if they had the will, which no one did.

It was the fifth of September when they crossed the border into Belgium. Along the way people were still dropping dead on the side of the road, pushed out of the line so they would not create a block for this arduous march. As they dropped Paul and Jean did everything that they could to help them, patching some injuries while on the march. They reached an enclosed compound made up of tents and tiny shack like huts, but it was the guard towers that loomed overhead like giant sentries that seemed to keep everything peaceful. A fence made of wood and wire stood ten feet into the air, wrapping everyone inside with its coldness. So, this was where they were to be held, somewhere on the French-Belgian border. Winter would be fast approaching, a fearful expectation of the things to come drifted through everyone's thoughts and into the air like a ghost. It hovered until it was noticed by everyone. They were herded inside in four lines that appeared to stretch beyond the horizon. It took days, people were dying. Eventually everyone was processed; name, birth, profession. Paul and Jean were both classified as prisoners of war, army medics and scavengers. They tried to explain that they had been providing medical treatment to both sides during this war. The Prussians viewed them as enemies and the French viewed them as traitors. They were placed in separate barracks. They both knew that this was going to be a trial, a trial unlike any they could ever have imagined. They met every day in the yard between waking and bread. Everything that they experienced they talked with each other about. They were experiencing a paralyzing sense of dread, a cold fear of what could come. If not for each other, the thought of being able to make it through this was just a bad idea.

The following morning Jean was called to meet with the camp commandant.

"Sind sie Arzt? Asked the commander.

"Ja, ich bin Arzt." Jean replied.

"Komm mit mir."

As they walked across the compound Jean could see green and blue fields off in the distance. Jean had seen nothing like it since visiting home. On the backside of the compound there stood a makeshift field hospital. There were other prisoners working in there, army medics, launderers, and anyone trained as a servant. This was the best that they could do, but it was much cleaner than a battlefield. The opportunity to perform a proper surgery enticed Jean beyond anything he ever experienced. A true test of skill, and emotional control.

Up to that point the army had treated the prisoners well, but the guards here were of a different sort, the sort that has no honor.

There were sick, injured, and dying Frenchmen all over the camp, so Jean agreed. Later that day Paul was called, he too agreed.

The following morning, they met at the medical facility. They were fed a little better than those in the barracks. They could not contain their excitement about this opportunity for some serious medical practice, but they had to contain it. Patients were lined up, but their first was a Prussian officer that had been grazed by a bullet across the back of his head. He was not hurt, not seriously, two stitches to the scalp closed it up. He kept saying "Danke, danke." When they had finished the officer said to Paul "Du bist sehr nett." Paul had no idea what this meant.

Next, they had a French officer that had been

wounded at Sedan. He had been shot in the forearm. The bullet was still in him and infection had already set in. It was bad, the only way to save him was to take his arm. Jean and Paul reluctantly gave him the news, which he did not take very well.

"I swung my sabre with this arm, I commanded hundreds of men into battle with this arm. How can I possibly go on without it?"

"Sir, going on without it is the only way that you will live."

"Then I will not live."

"Get some rest sir."

They walked out of the room, followed by the Prussian guard that oversaw their every move. They walked outside and the guard was never more than a step and a half behind. They discussed what to do about the French officer. They debated on this issue for a short period of time, deciding that they had an obligation to save someone's life, if it was within their capacity to do so. They went about their business for the next several hours before making their way back to the French officer. As the two sat down bedside, the officer began to speak.

"Boys, I am from Paris, from a well-to-do family, with land outside of Paris. After my education at the university I went to Italy for military school. There I met and fell in love with a married woman. Her husband was the conductor of the church choir in Florence, a prestigious position. This would have been a scandal. I could never have her for myself, it broke my heart. Although I loved her, leaving her was the best thing that I could do for her. I would not see her humiliated. I left

Italy and have never went back. That was the hardest thing I have ever had to do, losing my arm will be easy in comparison."

"Thank you, sir," Paul said. "If there was any other way…"

"I know," he said, interrupting Paul. Raising his arm, holding it up in a way that said, "Be quiet." He looked at his arm and said, "I know. Thank you, boys."

"Yes sir," they replied.

That evening they gave him a glass of water with a powerful sedative in it, opium. As he drifted off in what appeared to be a peaceful slumber the two got him ready. They had cleaned and sterilized all their surgical tools, as well as the officer's arm.

"Tie him off," Paul said, as he grabbed a scalpel. All the prep work had been done. He bent down and said a prayer, "Guide my hand O' Lord, make me strong as only your spirit can."

"Remember when you had gotten sick about eleven years ago?"

"Yes, I remember. But why…."

"Shhhhh, I thought we all might lose you, we all did, at least we all knew that it was a possibility. I am scared right now, but I have never been more scared than I was then, not even when we were captured."

"I know, I do not remember everything, but I remember enough."

After their short conversation they realized that Paul had made the incision and exposed the bone. Jean swapped places with him and began to saw through the bone.

"Why would you ask me about when I was sick, what's on your mind?"

"It's just that I do not really have any idea what's going to happen here, I mean..."

"Try not to think about it, just assume that everything will be fine," Paul stated, a might forcefully.

"I just wanted you to know..."

"I know Jean, you love me as your brother, and I you, but let us focus on the job at hand."

Jean had made a clean cut through the bone. They worked as a synchronized unit. That did not come from education, it came from a lifetime of experiencing every thought and feeling of each other. It was the perfect combination of knowledge and anticipation. This went on, even without Jean and Paul realizing it. They completed the operation without a hitch, as they were confident that that would be the case. Leaving the officer alone to recover, the two of them stepped outside, with their guard in tow. They felt a degree of satisfaction that the surgery was flawless, even more so that the officer agreed to it. If he had not, he would be dead inside of a week's time. They wondered if their talking with him had to do with his changing his mind. It did not. This officer was the kind of man that made up his own mind. He had been around for too long, seen and done too many things for his opinion to be swayed. Officers did not become officers by questioning their own decisions. No, this man decided on his own what he would do, then he would do it.

The following day they went in to see the officer, he had awakened a few hours earlier. He was in surprisingly good spirits.

"How are you today, sir?" Paul asked.

"Just fine young man, just fine."

They gave him an ointment to keep rubbed on the wound to minimize the risk of infection.

"I believe that he is going to be fine." Jean said.

"Yes, I believe he will."

Winter was approaching, they knew that they would be busier this time of year. There was not enough blankets, food, or morale. A barracks had been set up outside the medical facility for all the workers, it was warmer, they got better provisions, but seeing one patient after another was long, arduous work. Jean and Paul found it to be quite rewarding, it was a great experience amid a bad one. Medicine had become their lives. In a POW camp medicine was all that they had going for them. They felt as if their lives had meaning if they could save someone else's life. The following day they were given another of those not so rare opportunities. A young Prussian officer was brought in from a bullet in his chest and pneumonia, he was in more danger from the pneumonia than from the bullet. He must have come from a prominent Prussian family to have become an officer at such an early age. He appeared to be in his early twenties. The two of them worked through the night to save him, whether, or not he would live weighed heavy on their minds. They began by removing the bullet from his chest. It had hit his sternum and ricocheted to the right where it now sat precariously against his lung. They were able to get to the bullet without breaking any of his ribs. That was easy enough, pneumonia is something else entirely. They lit candles and placed them on his chest to try and dry out the pneumonia. In three days' time he was up and healthy as ever. They told him to take it easy so as not to rip the stitches in his chest.

"Are you soldiers?" He asked Jean and Paul.

"No. We are doctors, we have never been soldiers."

"Why are you here then?"

"We were on the battlefield at Sedan tending to the wounded when the army took us into custody." Jean said.

"Well, I'm glad that you are here, you saved my life. There are many more of my countrymen on the way here for medical treatment."

"Does your army not have their own doctors?"

"Yes, but they are ill equipped to handle the flood of injured soldiers." This troubled Jean and Paul, especially Paul. That night, while lying in their barracks, the two of them discussed this matter.

"Is that what we are here for, to treat their wounded when this camp is full of sick and wounded Frenchmen?" Paul asked.

"I agree," Jean said. "Yet practicing medicine means more to me than any other issue."

"I guess you are right, but I do not like the idea, it feels immoral."

"It's not immoral from a medical standpoint."

Paul struggled with this all night while Jean slept quiet as a baby. This was more than just a struggle for Paul, it was a dilemma. Jean immersed himself in his practicing medicine. Paul was being torn between his love for medicine and his sense of morality. He loved being a doctor, practicing medicine fulfilled him, but he did not like being told who to treat. That was the immorality of it, he could not work under compulsion. Paul often thought of Michelle, wondering how her life in Paris was going for her. He missed her terribly and he wondered whether she missed him. He would never forget that day he saw her dancing on the stage, such a vision of loveliness he had never seen.

That night a group of about a hundred Prussian soldiers arrived, every one of them in need of one form of medical attention or another. The alarm sounded waking everyone in the medical barracks. Everyone hurried to their post, everyone but Paul. He had gotten to the point that he would not be bullied into service. The soldiers suffered everything from battlefield injuries to dysentery. Paul and Jean did everything that they could, but Paul's heart was not in it. After thirty-six hours of tending to the wounded the medical staff had to take a break. It was late at night and the two of them walked outside to get some fresh air. They noticed some activity at the far side of the yard. They walked closer until a guard stopped them, but not before they noticed the burial of several French dead. They could not believe what they had just seen. Some part of them knew, another part wanted to ignore it. They did not talk about it that day, or the following one. It was tormenting them inside in its own personal manner. On the third day Paul told Jean that he had had enough. Jean disagreed with him for the love of medicine.

"I've had it!" Paul shouted.

"What about our plans to be surgeons?"

"You have to be human first, then, and only then can you make a moral decision. I will make my decision, as a moral man. I am that before I am a surgeon."

Paul stomped away from Jean at a quickened pace. When it was time for their shift to start Paul did not show up. Guards were sent to his quarters where he was found leisurely laying on his bunk. The guards yelled something that Paul could not understand, he got up and was hit in the small of his back with a rifle butt, knocking him to the floor. He slowly got up and followed the guards. They led him into the surgery prep room, he happily followed. He dressed out for surgery then followed the guards to a table where a Prussian major was laid out on with a bullet hole through his abdomen. Jean smiled when he saw Paul coming, Paul did not smile back. He took his spot beside Jean and then he folded his arms in defiance.

"I'm glad to see that you changed your mind."

"I haven't." Paul replied.

Paul ignored every action, every question, and most of all the patient. A guard tried to motivate him by hitting him in the back with the butt of his rifle. Paul fell to the floor.

"No." Jean yelled.

Paul stood up, crossed his arms and said, "If I cannot help everybody then I will help nobody."

"Paul, what are you doing?"

"I made up my mind, I am not going to be their fool."

"This is our living." Jean said.

"No, it is theirs." He said pointing out the guards. That earned him another rifle butt to the back.

"Drag him outside now." The commander of the guards ordered. Three guards grabbed him, took him outside and gave him a sound beating. Jean tried to follow but was held back by the guards that supervised them. A guard stood there with him while the others fetched the camp commandant. When he arrived, he apologized for the beating that his overzealous guards meted out. Paul knew it was the commandants doing, nothing at that camp happened without his say so. "So, they tell me that you do not wish to do surgeries anymore, is that true?"

"No sir. The truth is that I won't."

"Surely there must be something we can do to work this out."

"Yes. Let us start treating the prisoners." Paul said.

"This is out of the question, they are only prisoners."

"So am I. They are Frenchmen, and humans just like you and I."

"No, no it is not possible. There are too many injured Prussians that must be taken care of."

"Not by me, not anymore."

"Do you not enjoy your better accommodations?"

"At what cost?" Paul asked.

"Very well, we can do this your way. Guards, throw him in the barracks."

He was dragged off to general population and beaten along the way. After dragging him the last three hundred yards to the barracks, which felt like an eternity, they kicked the door open and through Paul in.

"Find him a rack." The guard growled.

A couple of men picked him up and carried him to an empty bunk.

"Half rations." The guard yelled. "See how that suits you, doctor."

No one was getting enough food as it was, half rations and men were going to start dying. Paul knew that he could help, but for now, lying on his bunk, he was too beat up to help anyone, including himself. He could hear the men muttering about him. Complaining that it was his fault that they were down to half rations.

Days after, when he finally awoke and had enough strength, he would go out and walk the yard alone to try and get his strength back, and to wrap his mind around his new situation. It was all coming to him.

One night while lying in his bunk he was attacked by several of the prisoners, one of them managed to stab him in the hip. They yelled "traitor" as they attacked him. A large group of prisoners were about to join in and beat Paul to death, when an old familiar voice from the back of the barracks yelled, "Stop." Everyone froze as the old man walked up.

"How are you doing Paul?" The old man asked. "Let me have a look, you will be fine, I'll see to that." The old man turned to the prisoners and yelled at them, "You idiots do you know who this is or what he has done? No one touches him." They all bowed their heads as if in shame.

Paul never expected to see the old sage again and now the old man had saved his life. Paul and the old man walked the yard together everyday conversing for hours on end. Paul tried to explain the difference between his course of action and Jeans. The old man told Paul that neither of them were right, nor wrong.

"We all have to do what drives us, Jean is doing what drives him, just as you are doing what drives you."

"Why did I see you taking valuables from dead soldiers?"

"Did that surprise you?"

"Well, yes it did."

"I told you when we met that I did what I wanted to do and sometimes what I did not want to do."

"I did not know that was what you meant."

"Well, a misunderstanding on your part does not make me wrong!"

"No, it does not. As a matter of fact, I have been experiencing that for months. For the first time I am torn between doing what I want and doing what I do not want. I do not like it."

"No one ever does son, but it is part of who we are from the cradle to the grave."

"Sir, I do not understand you."

"Ah, yes you do, all too well. It's your mind that you cannot wrap around, yet you are still the bravest man I've known, your brother Jean too."

"Jean too? How can you say that when he is working for them?"

"He is not working for them; he's working for him."

"Why must you always talk in riddles?"

"It's no riddle. Do you think that the road he is on is not fraught with its own perils? And he is very aware of it. Because you do not know his dangers, you should not try to judge what kind of man he is. Because he does not agree with you is merely a difference in principle, not love.

That is your brother, and he always will be."

Paul had more to chew on mentally than he ever did in med school. In school life was simple. A cadaver can be dissected, and that life described to the letter. The living, there is no way to know them, only their functions. As people there is diversity of thought, action, and belief. The dead suffer none of this. The old man was right, it was not right to be mad at Jean because of a choice that Paul made. Jean made his choices too. Paul wanted to see Jean and have a talk with him. They sorely missed each other's company.

-7-

Jean's days were long and tedious. Being the only real surgeon, or doctor, he was working thirty-six-hour shifts. He missed Paul terribly. He knew that they had beaten him and dragged him away. He truly did not know if Paul was alive or dead. Every day he would work on patients anxiously waiting on some word from Paul. Up to that point there had not been one. There were no Frenchmen coming in or out. No one to hear a word from. One day while on the yard Jean was approached by one of the Prussian guards, who handed a letter to Jean, it was from Paul "Your brother would like to see you."

"When?" Jean asked, not able to keep the look of excitement from his face.

"Right here tomorrow evening," the guard replied. "I never saw you, understood."

"Understood, I'll be here," Jean said.

Jean went back to work, but he could not stop thinking about Paul's being alive. All it takes to regain concentration is a mistake, Jean could not afford to make one. So, Jean got his head back into what he was doing, containing the excitement that he felt. As he turned to walk away, he slipped in a puddle of blood. He fell straight to the floor, landing on his left side and getting covered in blood. He stood up and looked around and all he could see was blood everywhere. He was not appalled at the sight of blood, but he did realize what a low value had been put on it.

The following day when Paul and Jean were to meet, the old man had gathered hundreds of prisoners into the yard so no one would notice Jean and Paul talking. The two met in the middle of the crowd. After exchanging a hug and many tears they pulled themselves together. Paul told Jean that his intention was to give medical treatment to the prison population, all of whom are being neglected, Jean agreed.

"Jean, I need you to get me a few things."

"Sure Paul, whatever you need."

"I need ether, antibiotic, syringe, scalpel, forceps, and a bone saw."

"Jesus Paul, I cannot just walk out with that much stuff."

"I need these things, even if it takes all week."

"Okay, I'll see what I can do."

They parted into the crowd which slowly started to dissipate. It took a little over a week to get the items that Paul asked for, but he did get them.

Jean's duties carried on as usual, while Paul tended the prisoners. Paul's accommodations were not as comfortable, or clean, but he did the best he could.

Jean had a patient come in, a very fat Prussian

officer, a colonel that had been shot in the thigh. Apparently, he was a well-respected and well-liked officer. He was given every attention. The bullet entered the top right thigh from an outside angle. Because of the officer's massive form, the bullet hit the bone and stopped. Jean put the officer under and cut into the thigh of a man that was more like a mountain. There were seven other officers standing by, including a general. Jean was used to this kind of pressure, it did not bother him at all. He could just as well have been teaching a class, explaining what he was doing and why. He had to cut several layers down so that the forceps could even reach the bullet. Then he sewed it up one layer at a time, there were six layers. When the big Prussian had awakened, he was so impressed with the work Jean had done, perhaps saving the man's leg. He pulled Jean down to him and said, "My boy, you did it!" Jean found himself to be repulsed at this fat man's praise. His compulsory service was taking a toll on him. He was consoled knowing that Paul was treating the prisoners and that he had a hand in that, not as active as he wished, but a part none the less, and that afforded him a measure of satisfaction. He tried to stay focused on his work, practicing medicine was the only thing that made him happy, or in this case satisfied. He did not see Paul very often, but he always thought about him. When they would have a chance meet on the compound, they would discuss the cases that they had to deal with. There were many, everyday there were many.

Paul often thought about Michelle, he missed her terribly. He may have already been with her if it had not been for this war, one which he had not endorsed, or was even asked about. He would lay awake at night sometimes and look at the moon and the stars, he wondered if she might be looking at them and thinking of him. He could see her face and feel her presence in everything of beauty that he saw, in the snow, in the wind, and the blades of grass that sustained most of the life on Earth. She was everywhere, but always with him.

Life in the prison camp was not getting any easier, but it was becoming more routine, which that alone made it more bearable. There is a measure of comfort in familiarity. Paul had a more regular flow of patients than Jean did. Soldiers were delivered by train, and by wagon, Paul's patients were residents at the camp. He worked on as many patients as he could, but he was constantly running out of supplies. The pipeline between Paul and Jean could only deliver so much. Paul was getting ether, bandages, and antibiotics from Jean once a week, it still was not enough. The prisoners had begun to trust Paul, and to an extent Jean. They could see that they were trying to help them as much as possible. Jean they still viewed with an uncertain eye because he gave medical attention to the Prussians. Most realized that if he did not give them attention Paul would not get the needed supplies to help them. Day after day passed and the number of prisoners that could now walk or move an arm because of Paul's work was steadily increasing. When Paul would walk on the yard people would say, "Hi doc," or "How are you today Paul?" Slowly he earned not only their respect, but their trust as well.

Many of the prisoners were still dying, there were

upwards of thirty-thousand prisoners of war at this camp alone, they could not all be taken care of, and the Prussians made no effort to see that they were. At night in the barracks the prisoners would tell war stories and drink wine that they had made from whatever fruit was available to them. They had removed a few of the floorboards, they would put their wine there to ferment. When it was ready it felt like Christmas, everyone became joyful. It was the one thing that the prisoners had to look forward to, other than their eventual release. Many held out no hope of that. The guards had begun to change the routine of the prisoners, to create confusion, it was working. They were fed later, then earlier, sometimes not at all. They were rounded up at odd hours and herded out into the yard, there was no reason for this, it was simple harassment.

Paul had become good friends with the sage old man. In this trying time, it helped to have somebody that he could confide in, share his fears with, anybody. He was a storehouse of knowledge and he told great stories. He had been a prisoner of the Prussians before, during the Austro-Prussian war. He was on the battlefield at Koniggratz when he was taken prisoner. He was there praying for the dead. Paul was quite sure that he was lining his pockets as well, but it did not matter, Paul had come to understand the old man, in some cases even agree with him. In Jeans absence Paul had someone he could confide in with the old man. Jean still confided in Paul about once a week when they would meet on the yard. At other times, he confided in no one.

News had arrived that the French had capitulated

since the capture of Napoleon the Third. This led the way to the French Third Republic. Metz had been captured. Paris had been captured which gave rise to the Paris Commune who had seized control of the government, they intended to keep fighting the Prussians, and establish a new government, even though the war was all but lost. They ruled from Paris for a few months until they were bloodily suppressed by the regular French army. There was a lot of bloodshed in Paris at that time and Paul was worried sick about Michelle. He tried as hard as he could not to imagine what may be happening in Paris. There was a lot of political fighting, which Paul did not understand, politics was never his forte, but he could not stop himself from thinking about Michelle.

Paul and Jean had met on the yard and Jean informed him that he would no longer be able to bring him medical supplies. Technically the war was over, but with the establishment of the Third Republic the war continued, albeit to a much lesser degree. Thousands were being killed in Paris every day. The soldiers were rounding up Communards and executing them, men, women, and children. The prisoners stayed in the prisoner of war camps that were spread out around Belgium and Luxembourg. Because no formal treaty had been signed the prisoners had not been released. At that point, the guards made no attempt at restraint. They were trying to dishearten the French so they would never want to fight the Prussians again. Public executions and torture within the camp became commonplace. No one wanted to die so everyone was on their best behavior, it did not help. The executions were not for punishment, they were a deterrent. Many of the prisoners that Paul had tended to and had become friends with were executed or tortured. Some were hung up with their hands behind their backs, bending their shoulders out of the socket. These scenes were placed at random locations throughout the camp. It was difficult to sleep with the moaning of those being tortured carrying on throughout the night. It was an incessant droning sound that made one's skin crawl. Everyone wondered if they would be next.

The guards would often toy with the prisoners. They would call them out of the barracks as if they were to be tortured or executed. Then they would beat them a bit and let them go. It kept all the prisoners on edge and in fear for their lives. Paul had reached a point that he just did not care, he refused to live in fear.

Jean was still working for the Prussians, he lived in fear every day. One mistake and there was no telling what punishment he may receive.

The winter had just passed. Butterflies were in the air searching for the tender blossoms of early spring. The prisoners were happy to see the sunlight again. They would go into the yard and play soccer with a pillowcase that they stuffed with whatever they could find. An armistice had been agreed upon by the two nations, but there still had been no formal treaty, so the prisoners remained.

Paul had continued treating as many as he could with his limited resources. One kid, younger than Paul, had a bullet removed from his shoulder and had regained full mobility in his arm. This was noticed by one of the guards, that night the kid was dragged from his barracks and interrogated in an attempt to find out who was the one that had fixed him, but he refused to give Paul up. He was beaten throughout the night. His screams of pain could be heard throughout the camp. Many cried, knowing that tomorrow it may be them. The following day he was brought out into the middle of the yard and shot. That night Paul cried throughout the night. He knew that he was why the kid was shot, but he also knew that he had an obligation to heal anyone he could, by any means necessary. This young man had looked up to Paul, he had even decided that he wanted to go into the medical field, just like Paul, once they were freed. He had fire red hair, which was unique among Frenchmen, but not defiling. The kid had come from a good family in Charleville. His mother had been a nurse during the Austro-Prussian war. She was herself Austrian. She had witnessed the inhumanity of war, but it was her pride in the part she played in the war that made this kid want to be proud of his own effort in war, especially for France. His father was a French cook. He had worked in one of the finest restaurants in all of eastern France. Paul wept for the kid's family as well. He was reminded of Luc and having to bring his body back to his parents. What a sad day that had been. Paul knew that these tragic events would never leave him as long as he lived. Things once seen can never be unseen. He did not know if the burden of guilt should lay on him, but it did. No one interrupted him as he cried, no, everyone felt his pain. Everyone took this tragic event to heart. This kid had been the youngest prisoner of war in the camp. He had survived the war, only to be murdered by the Prussian scum that interned them, and during an armistice. This event solidified the prisoner's hatred of the Prussians.

The following morning Paul asked Jean to quit giving the Prussians medical treatment, Jean refused. Then Paul demanded it. This was the popular opinion among the prisoners, Paul's decision had nothing to do with the popular opinion. His decision was based upon his own hatred of what he was enduring at the hands of their captors. It was his decision alone.

"If I were to refuse them medical attention, I don't know what they might do to me, or you.""They can do nothing to me, as for you, you might have your dignity back!"

"I have my dignity!" Jean barked.

"No, you have become their dog. They hold your dignity out to you like it is a bone that they will not let you chew."

Jean turned his back to Paul and stomped off in a fit of anger. Neither of them had ever spoken that way to the other. Paul felt bad afterwards, he could not believe that he had said that to Jean, although he had meant every word. He knew that a line had been crossed that there could be no coming back from. The last thing he wanted was a rift between himself and Jean, although that now appeared to be inevitable. It was as if over twenty years of their friendship disappeared in a matter of seconds. It was a feeling that could never be shaken. Paul carried on, as did Jean. During this time of their internment Paul continued to make friends, while Jean continued to make enemies, on both sides of the fence. Paul had met, in one way or another, every prisoner on the compound, and everyone treated him with respect. The experience of having friends other than Jean was new to him. He realized just how inexperienced he really was. The inexperience did not frighten him, the experience did. It did not feel right to have any measure of enjoyment that Jean could not be a part of. He needed him to share in life's triumphs, and to help hold him up through its tragedies. No matter how hard he might try to shake these feelings, his conscience would always remind him. Only Michelle had abducted his heart, she was the first person that he had ever had true feelings for. However, no one knew him as well as Jean.

There were no letters allowed in or out, so any communication with loved ones could only be yearned for, but never realized. Paul wanted to let Michelle, as well as his parents, know that he was alive and well. He wanted to tell his mom and dad that he loved them and to thank them for everything, which was something he had never done. He wanted them to tell the old baker that he missed him as well as the best pastries in the world. It was to remain as thoughts and feelings, unfulfilled. Paul dreamed of what he would do if ever he was to leave there alive, but he was prepared not to.

Jean often thought of home and the purple fields of lavender along the Meuse. He thought of Claudia only once. He did not love her, and he knew she did not love him. He did not harbor any animosity towards her, but he believed that he had given up his innocence because of her lust, and his own desire for experience. If he did not have experience before, he certainly did now, but not in the manner that he had ever imagined. It did not make him feel wise as he imagined it would, it only made him feel used up. The weight of the world weighed heavily on their hearts.

-8-

Michelle had written several letters to Paul at the home of his parents. She missed him terribly and wondered why she had not heard from him. She knew that he would never neglect answering her many letters. If his parents knew anything about him, she believed that they would have written to inform her of his condition, or of their extreme misfortune. Deep down she knew that something had happened to him. She harbored thoughts that he was dead which she shook from her mind as if they were simply flower petals that had gotten caught in her hair. As it was, she was left aching in her heart.

Claudia had joined with the communards, Michelle had not heard from her in some months, but she had heard about the arrests and executions. She prayed that Claudia was not among them. She never cared much for Claudia's behavior, she did not like it at all. Claudia was a bit too free with herself, always rebelling against the norm. Anything that was new, or controversial, Claudia would find herself drawn to it. They had been friends for most of their lives and Claudia always listened to her when she needed someone to talk to. Now there was no news of Claudia or Paul. She felt like her life was closing in on her. Her training at the academy had been going so well for her, but much like Paul's doctorate, had been put on hold due to the war. She still loved to dance, to sing, and to act. Many nights when she was alone in her room she would pretend to be dancing with Paul. Her arms extended, she would twirl around the room, eyes closed, imagining Paul holding her tight, spinning with her. This would go on for several minutes at a time, until she opened her eyes and felt like a fool, she would tell herself that she was honing her craft, a lonely heart-broken fool. She would lay in her bed at night and sing softly to her memories of him. She wondered what it would be like when the two of them made love. She cried because she feared that it may never happen, she may never see him again. She thought about his mom and dad and how much they must be missing him. Could they possibly miss him as much as she did? She decided that they did in a parental way. One thing that she was sure of was that neither of them wanted him out of their lives. No, that was something that neither of them could fathom. Michelle did not go out of her room very often, Paris had become an extremely dangerous place. She had confined herself to an eight by ten cell with a window and a small orchid sitting on its ledge. A pseudo justice had taken over that allowed for rape, theft, starvation, and murder. She believed that's what war was, anyway, murder, from both sides of a struggle. Each side claimed their own reasons, or justification, but to Michelle it was all just madness. What was once passed as justice flowing smoothly through the sea of humanity had been replaced with a swirling cesspool of violence, imposing itself as if for the common good. No one needed to be told what was good for them, but everyone could see what was not. Art made her world bearable, now that was being taken away. Jean's and Paul's parents saw each other every day. Their mothers often went to the market together and their fathers still worked together at the foundry and often played various card and dice games on the weekend. Since Jean and Paul had not been heard from in about seven months the mood became more somber with every passing day. The weekend games had become fewer, and then they were gone altogether. They missed the camaraderie, but they missed their children more. They had talked about it a few times, but no more, it was too painful to bring up. After all the tears that had been shed by them, they saw no sense in talking about it. No one wanted to contemplate what could possibly have happened to their children during this war. Pain passed through them every day, it resided in their hearts and chilled them to their bones. How much longer could time go on without any word from their children, or about them. Letters from Michelle were piling up, so Paul's mother decided to write to her.

"Dear Michelle,
My sweet, sweet child. Paul had spoken to me about you many times. He is very much in love with you. Judging by your letters you must feel the same way about him. I wish I could say something to calm the storm in your heart, and in mine, but I cannot. I have not seen or heard from my Paul since months before the armistice. I know that what he was doing was good and pure, I believe that, I must, as do you. We should believe that he is still doing that. He will be back to us as soon as he can. He loves you with all his heart, I know that, and his father knows that as well. We look forward to meeting you and the time when we can all be together. Pray for our Paul and his safe return.

Love"

She felt good about writing to Michelle and she wondered why she had not done it sooner. It helped to communicate her concerns with someone else. It was still a reminder of her own pain, and she did not want to be reminded of that, but she would do anything for her Paul, even carry her own pain with dignity, and help others to carry theirs. Heartache surrounded the country, it could be seen on the faces of everyone. The entire town loved and prayed for Jean and Paul. They missed the two good-natured boys that had grown into fine young men. They were all so proud of them and they harbored no desire to be proud of them in memory only.

The old baker was getting up in years and feeling tired. There was flour dust in the air inside the bakery and the smell of sweet cakes and pastries wafted through the air and lingered. It could almost be smelled throughout the entire village. It was a smell that always brought Jean and Paul running to his door. He missed them very much and often found himself looking out the window and down the street, half expecting the two boys to come running just like they used to. He missed the fish and the lavender in the window. He often cried when he thought of those two boys. Tears would streak down the flour that had settled on his face and splash onto his table into a milky white puddle.

Lately he had not been feeling very well. There was a persistent pain in his side that was almost debilitating. He was told by a doctor that he had an inflamed pancreas. If he did not love to bake, he would retire. His bakery served as a shelter for him, a safe haven. It was also his connection to the past, as well as to everyone that he dearly loved. He and his wife started the bakery two years before she died. He had to keep feeling a connection to her or he would have died a long time ago. He did not have any idea how much longer he would be alive, but he wanted to see Jean and Paul before he died, at least one more time. He needed to tell them that he loved them as his own.

-9-

Jean was awaken early in the morning. A young Prussian major had come in for surgery. A bullet had shattered against his shin. The fragments had shattered in a circular pattern from the entry wound outward. He was in a lot of pain. The young major spoke fluent French, so communication between the two of them was accomplished with ease. During this preliminary meeting Jean forgot the major was Prussian, his French was that good.

"Please," he said. "Do not let me lose my leg."

"I will do everything I can to see that does not happen."

"Thank you. I believe that you are truly a good man."

"You just relax," Jean said. "I'll take care of you."

Jean was still being watched throughout every surgery. He had grown used to it, but he still did not like it. Jean imagined that after all this time performing surgeries for his Prussian captors that they would leave him alone. They never said why they stood over him, but they did it anyhow. Perhaps it was so that he could never forget who was in charge.

When the surgery was to begin Jean gave the officer the necessary sedative, within seven minutes the officer was unconscious. Jean started by cleaning the outside of the wound and the area around it. It was quite a wound, the bullet had left his shin broken. It was almost impossible to find the bullet fragments, but he knew that he had to remove all of it, if not the wound would become infected and this young officer would lose his leg, or his life. Jean had to open the wound even more to get to the bullet. He found the main body of it flattened against the tibia, or shin bone. That was removed easily enough. As he stuck the forceps into the wound his patient let out a small groan as the pain worked its way through the sedative. Jean grasped the bullet with the forceps and gently pulled it out. Its flat, expanded shape tearing at the flesh around it as it was extracted. For the first time in his medical career he became conscious of the smell of blood. He paused and looked up at the single bulb that hovered over the table and wondered how it put out enough light to perform any kind of proper surgery, yet here he was. He looked around the room, first at the eight Prussian soldiers laying in their beds recovering, then towards the open window on the far south wall. The window had been opened to allow the cool spring air to blow through the infirmary. Jean then glanced at the guard that was watching him. He stood there looking stoical, flat, empty, with his rifle slung over his shoulder. Jean wondered why the guard never said anything, or why he never looked away. Jean's observations were more for him to catch his breath than they were for the sake of satisfying his curiosity. He had been working on patients for going on twenty hours and he was exhausted. He stepped back up to the young major and continued. There was little muscle between the skin and the shin, so most of the fragments that had not been blown back out could be felt by hand. Jean made an incision radiating out from the main entry wound along the paths that the fragments took until he was able to reach the fragment. The fragment was then extracted, and the entire area was thoroughly cleansed. There were six fragments total, all were removed with surgical precision. As Jean reset the tibia, the patient released another small groan, but he did not wake up. thirty-two stitches later and the surgery was finished. It had taken Jean about two hours to complete, now he was exhausted, he had to rest.

As Jean went to sleep that night he thought of Paul. After all that, the two of them had been through together it was hard to imagine that he was doing this alone. He was still upset about Paul calling him the Prussian's dog, but most of all because they had always been on the same page, united, in thought and action. He missed his friend, but the difference of opinion, on any issue, left him feeling shocked. These months had been the longest that the two of them had ever been separated before. He fell asleep to thoughts of their childhood together. He remembered fishing in the river Meuse and running through the fields of lavender and farm grass. Tears welled up in Jean's eyes, then he was asleep.

Paul paced the floor of the barracks wondering when all this madness would end. The old sage came up to him smiling.

"What is troubling you son?"

"I'm not sure," Paul answered.

"We all face troubles, that does not matter. It is how we deal with them that matters."

"I know, I just don't know how to deal with it."

"Maybe I could help if you were to share it with me," said the old sage.

"I'm afraid that if we ever get out of here my relationship with Jean will never be the same." "It will never be the same," the sage said.

"What do you mean, why not?"

"You have both expressed your individuality. You are both doing what you believe to be right. You have a sense of fairness that outweighs your sense of medical responsibility. He has a sense of medical responsibility that outweighs his sense of fairness. Such as he has devoted himself to the craft. So, you must see that neither of you are wrong."

"I do not know if I can see it that way."

"You can if you take an honest look at it. See it for what it is, individuality, which is no reason for hate, that would be among the stupidest of reasons."

The mood was as dark as the sky that night, but at least the sky had stars, Paul could see no light.

"The two of you are so used to being one that you never learned to be two," the old sage said. "You must learn that being you and making your own decisions makes you an individual, that is about you."

Paul thought long and hard about the words of the old sage, he was a wise man. Paul finally realized that he had to come to terms with his thoughts, but he doubted whether he knew how. He still loved Jean, he had always cared for his well-being, even prayed for it. It was the thought that he believed himself to be more correct morally, that created his conflict.

"Paul," the old sage said. "You must try to put yourself in his position, while maintaining yours."

Paul did not get much sleep that night. He had stayed up thinking about how best to deal with his own thoughts and feelings regarding Jean. Then he started drifting back to a simpler time. He remembered when he was sick as a little child and Jeans depression over the possibility of something bad happening to Paul. He remembered their work on the farms. The green grass that they would lead the cows out to so they could feed. The fun they had playing pranks on their neighbors. Hanging fish up outside the door of the bakery, and how they had laughed when the baker came out and walked right into them. He started laughing right along with them. Paul recalled a simpler time when he and Jean were united in purpose and their friendship. Then Paul began to understand. He began to feel guilty for ever having had negative thoughts about Jean. Their love for each other had always overshadowed any difference of opinion or action. It was being tried because they had never had such a difference.

The following morning on the yard it was such a beautiful sky, the sun was shining bright, spreading its warmth to everyone. The sun was totally impartial, mankind would never pleasure itself to make such the case. The things in Paul's life that used to solidify his character now created confusion. After much thought and emotion Paul came to a place of inner peace and love, not just for Jean, but for everyone, but especially Jean.

"I understand now," Paul said to the old sage.

"You have always understood, but it was necessary for you to reach for it on your own."

"I have. I am not sure how I feel, but at least I understand."

"Good, but know this," the old sage said. "A storm is coming that will break many, but you it will devastate. There will be no escaping it, no running from it, only dealing with it."

"What kind of storm?"

The old sage often spoke in riddles and parables, Paul would have liked something more conclusive.

"The sky will turn black, blacker than the darkest night. There will be lightening and hail stones, unlike anything you will have ever seen before, and it will leave death in its wake. Then, after time, the sky will become blue again, and the fields green."

Paul still did not understand, but he figured that was all he was going to get. The sage was wise, even if often misunderstood, so Paul just decided to wait and see. Paul, being a patient man, waited, but how do you await the fulfillment of such a prophecy? Even the old sage could not interpret it, but he could recognize it when it occurred. This was all too unreal for Paul. He was not a superstitious man, religious, yes, pious, no, but not superstitious. He went about the rest of his day playing football in the yard. The number of times that he had set bones or relocated shoulders due to this game he could not count. Yet the fun and freedom of the sport could not be relinquished. It made everyone feel as if they were outside, playing for a championship. It was what they all looked forward to. Football and bread, and they could never get enough of either. They had acquired a football somehow and were now playing real games. The guards would distract the players by throwing bread on to the field and laugh as some of the players went after the bread. Paul hated being treated as a source of entertainment. The guards would also disrupt the crowd in this same manner. It would incite all assortments of language, fights, almost a riot once, but gunfire into the air stopped it before it began. Paul, along with a handful of others, started throwing the bread back at the guards. On the occasion that they could not reach the bread they would do their utmost to smash it into the ground with their heels. Although the bread was longed for, it came at a cost that some refused to pay. Once they had resigned themselves to a certain fate, they became free, there was nothing that could be done to them that they had not already survived in their minds. Paul reached out with his leg and slammed his boot down on another piece of bread, just as another prisoner was reaching for it. The prisoner looked up at Paul, it was Jean. Immediately Paul felt an overwhelming wave of guilt fully overwhelming him.

"I am truly sorry Jean."

Jean never said a word, he just stood up and calmly walked away. Paul could not believe what he had just done, more to the point, who he did it to. Now his heart truly ached. He wanted to talk with Jean, he needed to, but he knew that could not happen. For the rest of the day, and well into the night Paul sulked. He came to the realization that Jean could see this as his drifting away from him, intentionally. He wondered how Jean might feel about him now. Jean had seen the look on Paul's face, he knew that Paul meant nothing by it, at least not towards him personally. He could see that Paul would have taken it back if he could. What a burden of guilt to carry, but Jean had his own burdens. He did not like being at the mercy of his Prussian captors, but he hated even more that he felt like he had no choice. He silently cried that night in his bed. He thought of his home, his family, the old baker, everyone he loved, with the exception of Paul. He did not omit Paul as a form of punishment, on the contrary, he loved Paul very much, he was his absolute best friend. He never had known anything else. They were both going through the same things, just in a different way. How did a life that was so simple, so laid out, ever become so twisted? Was this based on a different point of view? Jean and Paul were both battling with the same demons. If they could just get together and talk for a little while they could clear this whole mess up, but they could not talk. The only person Paul could talk to was the old sage, Jean had no one.

In mid-May a treaty had finally been signed, the Treaty of Frankfurt. The prisoners were to be declassified and released.

The sage old man was walking on the yard with Paul.

"Remember Paul, a storm is coming unlike anything you have ever seen."

"How can that be? The war is over."

"Yes, and it has stolen many lives, but it is not finished."

Paul did not pay it too much mind. He was happy that the war was over, they would all be going home soon.

-10-

Jean was happy too. No more medical attention under compulsion. Most of all he wanted to talk to Paul. All these thoughts gave Jean comfort.

No one knew when they would be released, it was being done by barracks. So far two barracks had been released. It was a slow process, but no one expected the Prussians to be quick, especially for their sakes. It was about midnight when Jean's Prussian guard woke him up.

"You have another patient," he said.

"No, the war is over."

The guard left and was back in five minutes with the camp commandant.

"What is this I hear that you will not see another patient?"

"The war is over, my obligation as a prisoner is over!" Jean replied.

"I am afraid not. There is a man coming here, an important man, a field marshal."

"What is that to me?"

"Your freedom, or not."

Jean knew he was in a precarious position. They still held the reins in on him.

"Okay. When he arrives come and get me."

"You will come now."

Jean climbed out of his bunk and put his clothes on. He had never hated his Prussian captors more than now. He was led to the infirmary and told to begin prepping. As he prepped, he cursed to himself. He wondered how he got himself in this predicament, but he knew that it was because he did not do what Paul did.

His patient arrived within the hour. A middle-aged man with military decorations all over his coat. He was an otherwise healthy-looking man. Jean had him strip and put on a gown.

"Where sir is your injury?"

"It is on the back of my leg, an old war wound from our conflict with Austria."

Jean rolled him onto his back and saw the wound, it was horrendous, gangrene had already set in. The wound had been relatively untreated for over five years.

"Sir, was the wound ever treated?"

"No, just field dressed."

"This wound has an infection that will kill you if I do not take your leg.'"

"If you take my leg, I will kill you myself."

There were all manner of lesser officers standing by.

"Sir, this infection can spread throughout your whole body, if it does, you will die."

"Then you must prevent that. Remember, if I wake up missing a leg you will be shot."

This weighed heavy on Jean's mind. How to save someone that is essentially refusing to be saved. Jean gave the officer the sedative, within a couple of minutes he was out. All there was that he could do was clean and sanitize the wound. If the disease had entered his bloodstream then there was no helping him. The wound smelled terrible, which was typical with gangrene. Jean really did not know what to do.

Excitement was running rampant throughout the camp. Everyone was anticipating their arrival back home.

"I will not be going home, the end of this war is my fate. I told you that much when we met." The old sage told Paul

"I did not believe that you meant it."

"You did not believe me, but I know why, it is understood."

"Is that the storm that you see coming?" Paul asked.

"No, that storm is yet to arrive, but look out, it is on the horizon."

Paul gave little thought to storms, still thinking that the old sage was at least half crazy. Paul's thoughts were on Paris, Michelle. He had been long enough without any contact with her that anything could have happened, and he would not know about it. The idea of being with her again had kept him going, and sane. He was not going to give up on that now. He thought of home, not in the sense of being around his family, but in the sense of repose. He thought a lot about Jean, what he would say to mend their friendship, if it could be mended. He thought of he and Jean as children, running through the beautiful fields, fishing in the Meuse, and pranking the entire village.Paul knew that those days were long gone now, but he did not want his friendship to be gone as well.

Jean saw little that he could do for this officer, but he tried his best. He put on a mask that was filled with lavender to mask the smell of the infection, it worked, to a degree. Jean made a few small incisions around the wound and pus and bad blood flowed out. He was trying to find the extent of the infection. The further up the leg he went the more extensive the infection proved to be. He cut everywhere that there was a sign of infection, each time with the same result. There was nothing further Jean could do. He sterilized the wound and sewed it all back up. The officer was moved to a bed to recover. After two days he seemed to be improving, on the third day he started to run a fever. Jean rubbed him down with alcohol, but the fever just got worse. On the fifth day the officer died. His body was carried back to Prussia for a state burial. Jean was placed under arrest and forbidden to leave the barracks. He knew that this was not going to end well, he resolved himself that such was the case. He lay in his bunk that night remembering his life, Paul was in every part of it.

The next day all the prisoners were told to line up in the yard, as they formed ranks a military detail was leading Jean into the yard. No one knew what was going on or why. An officer stepped forward and said, "You have been convicted of murdering an officer of the Empire of Prussia."

"I did not murder anyone." Jean silently said to himself. He knew that any attempt at defense would be futile. Paul looked around in utter dismay, he could not tell if this was real or not. When he realized that the detail was a firing squad the reality of what was about to happen took hold. He noticed how blue the Prussian army jackets were, how green the hills on the next valley over were. His mind took him to many places, in an attempt to escape the horrors of reality that he had endured for far too long, and it was to culminate into a tragedy of inconceivable proportions. They stood Jean up and took ten paces back. Jean looked through the crowd until he saw Paul, then he smiled at him. All that Paul could remember was blackness, he could not remember the crack of the guns that were used to kill Jean. He was looking in on a false reality. Paul remained in a state of disbelief, screaming in his head in a deafening tone. The world went black and Paul died inside. All he could hear, or feel was an incessant humming that consumed him. It throbbed in his body until it sounded like the roar of thunder in his head. Numbness consumed him. Paul was not aware of how much time had elapsed, it could have been a day, it could have been a year, he would have never known. He awoke after an undetermined amount of time, repeating to himself, "I never said I'm sorry, forgive me."

The old sage was standing over him wiping his forehead with a damp cloth. He had been out for two days, muttering in his sleep about forgiveness.

"Are you all right?" He asked. "You are not sorry. You did what your conscience told you was right, that is nothing to be sorry about. You are in no need of forgiveness."

At night, while lying in his bunk, Paul began to cry, not silently, but out loud. No one in the barracks said a thing, other than Paul's crying it was completely silent. Everyone had come to love Paul, or at least have a great deal of respect for him.

It took a long time for Paul to come to terms with what had happened if he ever did. His mourning process began with rage, he wanted revenge for the death of his best friend. Realizing that that could never happen, it just was not possible, besides, he would not know who to hold responsible. The Prussian army? That was not going to happen. He chose himself, he would be responsible, and he would strive for revenge. He realized after quite some time that it was entirely internal, he had to come to terms on his own. A lot of his time was spent crying and wishing that Jean were still with him.

Later that same week Paul's barracks was released. As Paul was leaving a voice from behind stopped him, it was the guard that supervised the surgeries.

"I am terribly sorry for your loss, Jean was a good man that was put in an impossible position. There was no way he could have saved that officer, it was impossible. I wanted you to know how I felt and to let you know how Jean felt. He often spoke to himself about you, he talked of little else. He was truly your friend, and you were his."

"Thank you for your kind words," Paul said.

Paul left the camp with nothing but pain in his heart, he left alone. As he trudged along, he came upon the old sage.

"Mind if I walk with you a bit," Paul asked.

"I expect you to. Do you mind if we go the same way we came?"

"No, I do not. I am not even sure where I am going."

"Are you not going home?"

"Home will never be the same again. How could I possibly face everyone and tell them that Jean was killed in front of my eyes?"

"Because Jean's life has ended you wish for yours to do the same?"

"I do not know what I want," Paul said. "I guess I just want all of this to go away."

"Be patient and all of this will go away, but not by your doing, but by times."

They walked in silence for a while, Paul trying to take everything in. He was still in disbelief. He thought about the words of the old sage and tried to make sense of it. From the standpoint of reason, it all made perfect sense, but Paul was not dwelling in a place of reason at that time. His emotions had run so rampant that he was just mixed up, he did not know what to think or feel, inside was just a painful knot. He would start thinking about how to break the news to Jean's parents and he would begin to cry. The old sage never tried to stop him, or interrupt him, he understood.

A gentle rain started to fall, it struck Paul as the most peaceful thing he had experienced in many months. After several minutes, the two of them were soaked to their bones. Paul took off his jacket and gave it to the old man. The old man thanked him, and they continued on their way.

"I have always loved the rain," Paul said. "It is like God's own goodness covering everything."

"Yes," the old sage said. "That is exactly what it is."

"I used to pray all the time, it was something that Jean and I had made a habit of. Lately I have not been able to find the heart to do it."

"I know and understand what you are going

through, and so does God, even more so."

"Do you think that he understands how I feel, even if I blame him?"

"God understands everything and forgives everything. At your time of trouble when you do not want him is when he is the closest to you. We are merely humans. People blame God because they cannot place blame anywhere else, but the truth is that His shoulders are broad and His love enduring. People tend to only see the good when their lives are in order, it is when our lives are in disarray that we most need to see the good."

That left Paul with some serious thinking to do, but the truth was that no amount of thinking in the world could alter his irrational emotions.

They dragged themselves along a familiar path, it was the one that led to Sedan. As they passed the field of battle, they could see that it had been cleaned up, it still had giant potholes where the artillery had exploded, but all of the human remains had been removed. Paul could not see any difference, the scenes that he witnessed were forever scorched into his memory.

"Peace through war is a tumultuous peace," the old sage said.

"A tumultuous peace is like a powder keg," Paul agreed. "Do you think it will ever stop?"

"No, mans will to power is insatiable. It is a disease of his own making, once infected it cannot be easily overcome. I fear that war has become as much a part of man as breathing. We, as individuals, may find peace, as long as we search for it."

"Will I ever find peace?"

"Peace is not everything going great in your life, peace is dealing with loss, with life, and most importantly, dealing with yourself. You find a way to do that and you will have the peace that you need."

Walking along by a clearing that had a beautiful brook beside it, Paul tripped and scraped his knee.

"Are you alright?" the old sage asked.

"Yes, I am fine, just a little blood, nothing that I have not seen before."

"You are striving for something that you believe you will never find, but you have found a measure of it already."

"What is that exactly?"

"Reclaiming the part of yourself that was lost when Jean died."

"I will never be able to reclaim it, Jean was my brother."

"You are already reclaiming it. You will always miss him, and he will always be a part of you, but he is not you."

Not quite knowing the meaning of the old sage's words they walked along in silence for a while. They stopped at the spot where Jean and Paul had first met this old sage.

"This is where we say goodbye Paul."

"Why? You are the only friend that I have left."

"That is not true. Look around, there are many that love you, you just do not feel it, not yet, but you will."

"I still do not want you to go." Paul said.

"Paul, I told you when we met that the end of this war would see my fate, now it is time. That is precisely why we have stopped at this spot. Now help me over to those trees where I can lie down and listen to the birds sing to me once more."

After helping the old man off the path and into the woods Paul struggled with the words that he wanted to say. There was so much to tell this sage, but nothing came to Paul's mind except "thank you."

"Do you not see that you owe no one anything. Knowing you has been my blessing. Now, say a prayer for me, for Jean, and most importantly for yourself."

The old sage laid down right there and died. Paul sat there with him for two days wondering what to do, then a calm came over him, he listened to the birds, and the trees. He realized that there was much wisdom in this man's words. He prayed for the first time in many months. He said a prayer for the old sage and for Jean, he asked nothing for himself. He set off on the road to Montmedy. He hoped he could find food and possibly a bed. He had no money and no longer a belief in the goodness of people. He passed a field where a man was tending a herd of cows.

"Sir, do you know where I might find food and lodging for the night?"

"Can you work?"

"Yes sir, I can work," Paul replied.

"I will put you up if you can help me milk these cows."

"Yes sir, thank you sir."

They waited for the cows to finish grazing then they were led into a barn. Paul had fond memories of working on his uncle's farm when he was a boy. He remembered the summer that he and Jean both worked on the farm together, his throat started to tighten, but he kept his tears to himself. Paul had not felt much like talking or communicating in any way since the death of Jean. He would ask questions if he needed to know something, he would answer a question if asked, but he seldom went beyond that. He preferred to just keep to himself. In the past his only confidant was Jean, now with him gone there was no one. He enjoyed being in the field, it brought him joy and a sense of calm. He did not have to talk, or even think very much, he just was and that was the most comfortable for him at the moment. He knew that he would come to terms eventually, he just had no idea when or how. He worked the farm day in and day out, even having his meals alone. The farmer was a nice enough man and he had a darling little girl that was nine years old. After about a week the farmer approached Paul in the field and said, "Paul, my daughter and I would like it if you sat down to dinner tonight with us."

"I would not want to be any further burden than I am already."

"Burden? Do you know how difficult it is to get all of the daily work done on a farm?"

"Yes sir, as a matter of fact my uncle owns a dairy farm just outside of Briey."

"That is the most I have learned about you in a week," the farmer said.

"I apologize sir, I just find talking to be a bit depressing."

"I am sorry to hear that, but call me by my name, not sir, I am not your superior, so call me Max, and my little angel is Nicole."

Paul smiled for the first time in quite a while, he liked the way the smile made his face feel, it was relaxing, but it made his heart feel even better. He was not sure exactly what he was doing here, maybe just trying to figure things out, find where he stood with himself. He wanted to go home and see his family, but he did not have the heart to tell them about Jean's death, even though he knew that they needed to know. He blamed himself for Jean's death, if Paul never would have left him, he believed that Jean would still be alive. He was carrying a burden of guilt that was killing him inside. He missed Michelle and everyone else that he loved, this only added to his burden.

He decided to have dinner with the family and try to regain some sense of normality in his life. He had never been around Nicole and the only time he had been around Max was when they were milking or leading the cows out to pasture, so he thought this may be awkward. It was, but only for him. Max was more of a host than an employer and he seemed to enjoy the company. Paul guessed that he did not receive many guests.

They sat down at the table which had been set by Nicole. There was ham, bread, turnips, and sorbet. Paul had not seen a meal like this in a long time, and he was starving. Max said a short prayer thanking God for their food, the end to the war, and the company of Paul, which he believed that God had sent to him for some reason, one that he was not sure of yet, but he believed there was a reason.

"What is your name?" Nicole asked.

"My name is Paul."

"Mine is Nicole."

"It is a real pleasure to meet you Nicole."

"Nicole, give Paul some room, he works hard and must be hungry."

"No," Paul said. "I think that Nicole is wonderful company."

It was obvious that Nicole adored her new friend, and Paul adored her as well. Paul put a piece of ham in his mouth and it almost melted, it seemed like the most delicious thing he had ever eaten, next to the old baker's pastries.

"How old are you Nicole?"

"Nine years old," she answered.

"Nine, huh, but you are such a big girl."

Nicole cracked a smile that could melt stone. She was such a lovely little girl. Paul knew that she would grow into a fine young woman one day and make Max a proud grandfather. They finished their meal, and all sat satisfied.

"I will head out to the barn and see you in the morning," Paul said.

"You know, Paul, we have an extra room. There is no need for you to keep sleeping in the barn."

"It is no problem at all."

"Paul, I insist that you start sleeping in the house, it is far more comfortable."

"All right Max, if you insist."

Paul really did not want to sleep inside. He believed it would make him more endeared to this family and he did not want to do that. He was not sure how long he would be there, but he knew that he could not stay forever.

-11-

Days had turned into weeks and Paul's fear was becoming realized, he was becoming endeared to this family. Max had restored Paul's faith in the goodness of humans, at least to a degree. Max treated Paul as if he were part of his family, Paul was afraid of that. Nicole had become like Paul's little sister, even accompanying them into the fields to feed the cows. This was good for Paul, but he was still afraid of having feelings for anyone, it only served to remind him of Jean. He enjoyed the memories of Jean, but not the pain that they carried with it. He needed to talk about it, but he would not, the death of Jean was still too fresh in his mind, he could see it when he closed his eyes. He wished it would go away, but he knew that it never would. He thought of Michelle often, but he was not ready to see any one or renew his feelings, although he loved her. The weeks had finally become three months and by that time Paul felt as if he belonged on Max's farm. In the pasture one day Max started telling Paul about his history. The weather was beautiful, the skies, blue, and the fields, green, it called for such a conversation.

"I met Nicole's mother a little over twenty-five years ago. She was an absolute angel, the most beautiful woman that I had ever seen. We wanted children and we tried for years. We had given up on the possibility of it ever happening when she became pregnant with Nicole."

Paul could see the tears welling up in Max's eyes and tell that he was trying to hold them back. He could hear the crack in Max's voice and the emotional strain was seeping through. He started to feel sad for Max and at the same time realized that his tragedy was not the only one the world had seen.

"Her pregnancy went well, but when she was nearing the end of her pregnancy, she started having a lot of pain, and bleeding. She delivered my darling little Nicole okay, but she died while giving birth, she just could not stop bleeding." Max said, while reaching an emotional point that he was sobbing.

"I am so sorry Max, I never thought about the pain that is everywhere, it surrounds us. It tucks us into our beds at night and is there to wake us up in the morning."

"I don't know what I would do if I did not have my little angel with me."

"She is definitely a little darling butterfly."

Right then, at that very moment, an explosion from an undetonated shell rocked the field. Paul and Max both looked in the direction of the blast and saw Nicole lying face down in the field where she had been running towards them.

"Noooooooooo," Max screamed as he and Paul both ran to her. She was unconscious and there was a small splinter of metal shrapnel sticking out of the back of her head.

"Oh God, no, let her be okay," Max cried as tears poured down his face.

Paul picked her up and carried her to the house and laid her on the table.

"I need a razor, some clean rags, and some boiling water," Paul said. "Quickly."

Max was not sure why he was doing this, but he never questioned Paul, Paul was speaking with great authority. As the steam kettle whistled Max poured it in a bowl and brought it to Paul, along with the other requested items. Paul put the razor in the bowl, wet a clean cloth, and cleaned the blood from the back of her head. "Do you have any brandy," Paul asked.

"Yes," Max was back in a second with a bottle of brandy which Paul immediately opened and poured a small amount on the wound in the back of Nicole's head.

"What are you doing?"

"Do not interrupt me," Paul forcibly stated. "You might want to leave until I am finished."

"I will not leave my baby."

"All right, but please do not interrupt me, I know what I am doing."

Paul took the razor and shaved a small area of her hair away so he could get a better look at the wound. He then opened her scalp with a two-inch incision and saw the condition of her skull. It was cracked, but fortunately the shrapnel had not entered her brain. Paul removed the metal and asked for a needle and thread, which Max promptly brought. Paul sewed her scalp together with four stitches.

"Take her to her bed," Paul said. "Do not leave her. If she runs a fever let me know immediately."

Max disappeared around the corner of the hallway. Paul walked outside and burst into tears. He prayed for Nicole as she had become somewhat of a little sister to him. Yes, he loved her, and all his emotions that he had kept bottled up inside came charging out of him like a

Roman chariot. He had never experienced such a tide of feelings all at once and he did not know where he stood in the midst of it all.

For the next three days Paul tended the farm alone, he never even saw Max or Nicole. Choosing to take small meals from the barn, where he had gone back to sleeping.

On the fourth day, while out in the pasture Max came running up to Paul yelling, "She is awake, she is awake." Yelling while tears ran down his face. Paul fell to his knees clutching at his face thanking God for Nicole's speedy recovery.

Max reached Paul and grabbed him by the shoulders and lifted him to his feet hugging him, their tears intermingling on their faces.

"Paul, she woke up, hugged me around my neck and then asked for you. Will you go see her?"

"Yes, as soon as I get the herd back in."

"Do it now. The herd is not going to go anywhere. Come on."

They both ran across the pasture to the house. Down the hall and into Nicole's room. They found her sitting up on her bed and playing with a doll.

"Paul, I knew you would come to see me. I love you."

"I love you too little princess, Princess of Montmedy."

Max stood back while Paul and Nicole hugged, he cried while laughing like a schoolchild. He was so happy to see that his little angel was going to be okay.

"Now," Paul said. "Let me have a look at your

head."

Nicole smiling ear to ear turned her head to show Paul the back.

"It looks good, healing up nicely." Paul turned to Max and said, "In a couple of weeks I will remove the stitches and she will be completely healed."

Max fell to his knees grabbing Paul by the hands, he kissed them and said, "I knew that God brought you to us, I just did not know why, now I do. You saved my little girl."

"I did what I could," Paul replied.

Max did not know what to make of this, but he was pleased with the way it turned out. He was happy, confused, and he had feelings for Paul like he had become his son, and brother, yet his superior. Paul felt awkward about the change in the relationship between he and Max, he did not want to be viewed any differently.

After a week had passed everything was back to normal. Max and Paul were both tending the herd and Nicole was coming back out to the pasture with them. The two of them were sitting in the barn milking the cows when Max said to Paul, "I never properly thanked you for saving my Nicole."

"You do not have to. I am glad that I was here to be of help. Nicole getting better is thanks enough for me," Paul said.

"Nevertheless, you did not save only Nicole, you saved me too. You have become a son to me."

"I do not think I saved only you two, but maybe myself as well."

"Paul, how did you know what to do with Nicole?"

"I used to be a doctor."

"How are you so good with the herd?"

"I was born to farm, I have always loved the field."

"The way you treated Nicole says that maybe you were born to do something else, maybe to be a doctor."

"I am not a doctor anymore, I am a farmer."

"There seems to be a lot that you are not telling me Paul, but I will always be here to listen if you want to talk."

Paul said, "Max, I grew up in the village of Briey. I had uncles that owned dairy farms. That is how I came to know about the fields and the handling of dairy cows. My father worked in a foundry, he did not take to dairy work, I did, but my dream was to be a doctor. I went to medical school in Metz. After the war Metz ended up in the hands of the Germans, my training was cut short by the war."

"I am truly sorry that your dream came to an end, but if it had not then you never would have been here to save my Nicole."

"If I had not been here, perhaps she would have not been in the field when the explosion occurred."

"Paul, you look at the dark side much more than you do the light. Why?"

"I have never spoken about it, but my dreams were not mine alone. I had a friend that was dear to me, more so than a brother. We were raised up together, we did everything together. We even worked our uncle's dairy farm. We left our parent's home when we got through with secondary school. We were both accepted into medical school in Metz. We toured most of France before leaving for school where I met the only woman that I have ever loved, Michelle. I am still in love with her. With less than a year left in my studies the war broke out, our studies were put on hold. Jean and I left the university to follow the army and treat the wounded. We went from battlefield to battlefield treating the wounded on both sides of the conflict. The things we saw, the things we heard, things that I can never get out of my mind. At the battlefield of Sedan we were both taken by the Prussian army and taken to a camp for prisoners of war. There we were forced to give medical attention to the Prussians while Frenchmen in the camp were dying all around us from injuries that we could have treated. We agreed to treat their officers and soldiers, but I quit giving them medical attention when they refused to let us treat our own countrymen. Jean continued to treat the Prussians, much to my displeasure. It created a rift between the two of us, a rift that I was never able to mend. Jean was executed in front of my eyes. I could not believe it was happening, I never said a word, I just watched him die. Before he was shot, he looked at me and smiled as if he had made the peace that I could not. I came here upon my release. I have not been home, my parents and Jean's parents still do not know what has become of us. I do not have the heart to go home and tell them, nor do I have the heart to go to Paris and find my Michelle. I have not felt anything in months, I have been emotionally numb. Helping you and Nicole has been the first positive experience that I have had in a long time. I believed that I could never return to a normal life. Then you told me about your wife, and I see how you are with your daughter. You have done more for me than I could ever do for you. Your pain made me realize that life is not about experiencing pain, that is going to be given regardless of who we are, it is about the love we can show despite our pain. I have come to see that, but I have not reached a point that I can act on it, not yet. Someday I hope to be able to."

"Paul, I had no idea. I do not know what to say, but I do believe you to be among this world's great men. I have no doubt that you will do what is right and good in your own time. Know this, this is your home as well as mine and Nicole's, you are welcome here for as long as you live."

"Thank you, Max, you and Nicole have become very dear to me, for that I am forever indebted to you."

"Your indebtedness has been paid a thousand times over. Let us go inside and eat. Nicole has prepared something special with her own hands."

They had finished up in the barn and went inside the house where Nicole was already waiting on them. She had made a cake with sour cream and cheese.

"This is for you Paul, because I love you."

"I love you too little princess."

He dug into the cake with the greed of a starving man. It was not especially good, but it was special because it came from her with the words "I love you."

-12-

Paul had become settled into this new life, but there was a constant nagging in the back of his mind. He had been aware of it, as he had been aware of his attempts at ignoring it. He had become accustomed to the ease and simplicity of life on a farm. He would often get up a bit early and head out to the pasture with the herd. While they grazed, he would lie in the field on his back looking up at the sky, it was always so blue, impartial, and peaceful. He could stare at the sky and become mentally and emotionally vacant. No thoughts of who he was, what he had seen, or the pain that he had endured. Only the blue sky and the gentle clanging of cow bells, a sound which he had come to love. At noon he and Max would lead the cows by tens back to the barn and start milking. There were many jobs to be done on the farm and Paul knew them all. He loved this routine, it required little thought. Surgery, on the other hand, required thinking on your feet, and quickly. It was a difficult thing to do without any emotional involvement. You always cared for the well-being of your patients, that was a defining characteristic of a good surgeon, and a great man.

"Up early again Paul?" Max would ask, as he did every morning.

"It was such a beautiful morning that I did not want to miss any of it." Paul would answer.

"It looks as if it will continue throughout the day."

"Yes, it certainly does."

Even this small talk between he and Max was comforting. It helped to remind him of absolutely nothing. Nothing was exactly what Paul wanted to be reminded of. Nothing that caused him pain, nothing that reminded him of what he had lost, nothing that made him think about what could have been. He spent time in the evenings reading to Nicole. He enjoyed doing this, it was a new experience, it was not a reminder. Reminders are what Paul most wanted to avoid.

"We are going into town today to pick up some supplies, would you like to go with us?" Max asked.

"Sure," Paul said. "I have not even seen a proper town in a year."

"You are in for a treat. This town was relatively untouched by the war, although many of the young men had served with the army. Some made it back, many did not. The town has completely gotten back to normal since the war ended."

"Sounds good."

"We go into town once every couple of months to pick up some supplies, I usually buy Nicole something, a new doll, or a new dress, anything so that I can see her little eyes light up." Max said.

They hitched a team of horses to the carriage and headed off to Montmedy. It was a beautiful journey. The fields were a vibrant green and the forest off in the distance stood there like a defiant wall of green and brown. However, there was no lavender and that was a purple that Paul sorely missed. He held Nicole throughout the trip at her insistence. He made faces at her and told her little short stories. It really was a wonder to see her face light up as with a new discovery.

They arrived a couple of hours later. It was a relatively short ride.

Montmedy was larger than Briey, but it still felt like a small village. They parked the team outside of the town square and walked into the middle of town. There were children playing in the square with a little dog. The dog had a grayish brown fur with knots in it from being unkempt. It betrayed the puppy's age. The little boy had on brown trousers and a red shirt. The little girl wore a pink dress that was all but ruined from her handling of the dog.

"Can I play with them daddy?" Nicole asked.

Max looked at her, and then at the dog, then back at Nicole. You could read the indecision in his eyes. Damn it! He was supposed to be a father, not a mother.

"Go ahead sweetie," Max replied.

Nicole ran off to introduce herself to her new friends, she would play along with them and play with the dog.

"When was the last time that you were in a town like this?" Max asked.

"Almost a year ago. I was in Marsal to bring the body of a young boy named Luc home to his parents."

"I am truly sorry Paul."

"It's okay. I am trying to put all of these memories behind me."

"They can be behind you, but they will always be a part of who you are. I believe that you will always do the right thing."

"Would it be alright if I was to buy something for Nicole?" Paul asked, changing the subject.

"Sure, I think that she would like that."

Max went his way to take care of business, Paul went on a walk around town. He passed by the bakery, he liked the smell, but it did not compare to the bakery back home. His fond memories of that bakery were one of the things that made him crave his home. He could feel himself being pulled back there, yet he resisted. He walked along the main street. There were children playing down every alley and side street. Curtains in a window blew from a breeze that was coming from inside. They were a vibrant crimson, like the color of royalty. A woman stuck her head out of the window and yelled for her child to come home. Smells and noises were coming from everywhere, they covered over the muddy road. A pair of dogs were fighting over a bone outside the door of the butcher's shop. Sights that were very unfamiliar to Paul, but, made him long for home even more so. He walked along until he came to a shop that sold children's playthings. He walked through the shop slowly, looking at everything. There were dolls, bells, and ribbons of all colors, then he saw the perfect gift for Nicole, a stuffed lion. He bought it for her, hoping that it would make her happy. As Paul made his way back to the carriage, he passed Nicole, she was still playing with the other children and that smelly, dirty dog. He hid the lion from her. He did not notice her leaving off from playing with the other children and start trailing behind him. He jumped up and seated himself, then he noticed Nicole standing on the ground looking up at him.

"Will you help me up?" Nicole asked.

"I will," Paul replied.

Paul reached down and grabbed her by her outstretched arms and hoisted her up.

"There you go," Paul said.

"Can I sit here with you?" Nicole asked.

"Sure, you can, I was hoping that you would. I have something for you."

"What? Let me see."

Paul pulled the lion around from behind his back and handed it to Nicole.

"For me? I love it. I have never seen one of these."

She immediately began playing with it. She would make roaring sounds and pretend that the lion was stalking an animal that was being portrayed by her fingers.

"All done," Max said as he walked up to the carriage. "Supplies will be delivered tomorrow, and our produce will be picked up. We made a very handsome profit. Thank you, Paul."

Paul did not understand why he was being thanked for it, but he accepted it anyhow. His sense of social grace would allow him to do no less.

"Daddy, look at what Paul got for me," Nicole said with her eyes beaming.

"That is nice, a little scary though. He might eat you one night," Max said.

"Daddy it is just a toy. Right Paul?"

"Yes, dear he is only a toy, you might eat him."

Nicole laughed and said, "I will not, I promise."

"That is a good girl," Max said.

The carriage headed back off towards the farm. It was a slow, peaceful trip with little being said, but it was obvious that Max was enjoying the moment, it was written on his face, and Paul could read very well. It was clear he had something on his mind, something he was happy about. Whatever it was Paul was oblivious to it.

The trees seemed to grow in on the lane back to the farm. It brought to attention, in Paul's mind, the old sage. Paul had never thought about this man's wisdom.

His words started coming back to him, "Reclaim the part of you that died with Jean."

Paul was still lost in his thoughts when they arrived at the farm. He came to and let the cattle out into the field. It was already after noon so the cows could only graze for a short while. Paul led them out to the pasture, as he led himself out there too. While the cows grazed Paul laid down and looked up at the sky. The feeling to go home was bearing down on him and he needed this burden lifted. He already had his own burdens to bear, he could not bear the burdens of his and Jean's parents as well. He decided that it was time for him to go.

Before the sun went down Paul was heading back to the house. Dinner was on the table and Max was still looking pleased. They all sat down to eat.

"I would like to speak with you after dinner," Max said.

"Sure," Paul replied.

They sat there in silence as they ate. It was a delicious meal of bread crumb and cheese crusted veal. Paul thought to himself that he had not lived this good for a few years, at least since medical school. He was starting to see his way back to a happier life.

"Nicole, dear would you excuse us?" Max asked.

"Yes daddy."

Nicole left the room, but Max did not say anything for a moment, he sat there looking at Paul and smiling.

"Paul, I want you to know how much Nicole and I appreciate, no, depend upon your being here. Today at the market I doubled what I usually make," he said while sliding a leather pouch on the table over to Paul. "This is half of this month's profit, our production is doubled, that is your doing."

"No Max, I am only doing what I was hired to do. I said that I would work the herd for food and lodging, you have held up your end of it, I thank you for that."

"Paul, I want you to be my partner in this farm. There is no one that I would trust more."

"While in the field today I knew that I had to go home. I can no longer carry my parent's burden, or Jean's parents. I have to go home."

"I knew that you would find it in your heart eventually, you are a great man. Take the money, the offer for a partnership is always going to be open to you. You have earned this, and you will need it to travel."

"Thank you," Paul said with a small lump in his throat.

"I will see you in the morning."

"Good night."

-13-

When the morning came Paul was already gone. The idea of another goodbye was torturous, a torture that he was no longer willing to endure. These people had become family to him. Everything that Max did for him endeared him to this family even more. He hoped that Nicole would understand, he was going to miss her. He knew that he would see them again, sometime. He started the long walk to Briey. Along the way he thought about how he could possibly break the news about Jean's death. Paul needed peace, as did their families, this had to be done. Paul had walked all day, into the late afternoon, when he sat down to rest. It was along a beautiful wooded lane, that appeared as if it had been untouched. War had spread through the area of eastern France like the plague. Paul saw it as a miracle that this spot remained unmolested. This would have been a good place to hide during the war, but no one hid. Paul thought of the old sage and how much he appreciated nature. He was a man of much wisdom, and sorrow. Another life stolen from a world that could only have benefited from it.

After a nap and a bite to eat Paul set back out on the road. He paid more attention now to the world around him than he ever did before. Attention to nature, to people, to the things seen and the things unseen. He would notice a cricket in the grass, or a bird on a branch, things that in the past he paid little mind to. He still harbored doubts about going home, but it was something that had to be done, of that he had no doubt.

There were quite a lot of fields and wooded areas between Montmedy and Briey. Paul, for the first time, walked through them and felt peace at the beauty of what has been untouched by man. There was so little of it, it needed appreciation for its continued existence. Everything needs a degree of appreciation to survive.

He reached the outlying fields that he had been longing for. He laid down amongst the sweet lavender and slept until the morning gently began to warm his face. At that light he rose and brushed his hands through his hair to shake out the petals that had certainly gotten caught there over the night, and then he started walking towards Briey. As his mind started to go backwards his legs refused to go, they only went forward. He continued on until he had entered Briey. His mind was running faster than he could keep up with. His mind had reached the door of Jean's parent's house before his body did. He already knew what he would say, he knew how he would act in response to any given situation. When Jean's mother came to the door she burst into tears at the sight of Paul, everything that he thought he would do was forgotten. He began crying along with her. They stopped when the pain in their eyes quit burning.

"I am so glad to see you Paul, we did not know if we would ever see or hear from you again. I know that something happened to Jean, you would never have come here alone. Please Paul, tell me what happened."

"We were taken as prisoners of war. Jean died there."

"How? How did he die?"

"He died like a man, like a hero. Always doing what he knew to be right. He was executed for it. He gave medical care to those people that were in need, and he helped those that were not deemed necessary."

"Oh, how we have missed the two of you. Have you seen your mother?"

"No. I wanted to see you first, to let you know. I share your loss. Jean was my brother, he will always be in my heart."

She hugged Paul and crying said, "Come with me, let us visit with your mother."

They walked out of the house dependent on one another for support. When they arrived at Paul's parent's house, they looked at each other as if they did not know what to do. Neither knocked, nor said a word to the other, they just looked at each other. They were just standing there when Paul's mother opened the door, she screamed and then fainted. Paul caught her before she hit the floor, "Mom," he yelled.

She came to after a couple of minutes. She stared in disbelief at her son. She could not grasp the fact that he was really there.

"Paul, is it really you?"

"I am right here, just relax."

"We had no way of knowing what had become of you. Where is Jean? I knew the two of you would look after each other."

"Mother, Jean is dead."

"What? How?"

He explained to his mother and again to Jean's mother what had happened, but he never mentioned the riff that had become between them. He did not want their relationship to be remembered that way. He did not want to remember it that way.

"Where is my father?"

"He is at the foundry."

"Okay, sit at the table, I will get you some tea."

Paul heated up water for the tea while his two mothers sat at the table. They cried gently for Jean, and Paul cried to himself. He felt the pain of losing Jean as sharply, or even sharper than anyone. He was the only one living with guilt about it, that alone separated him. He served the tea and sat down at the table with them. He poured himself a glass of wine. He was on his third glass when his father got home.

"Paul, Paul, my God thank you. Paul where have

you been?"

His father fell to his knees hugging Paul, kissing him on his hands. Paul pulled him up.

"Father it is so good to see you alive and well."

They all rose and went over to the home of Jean's parents, where Jean's father and Paul's father were the only two that were uninformed. The women set the table and Paul noticed everything, the red and white striped tablecloth, the smell of a goose roasting, the quiet lucidity that came before sharing something of such great magnitude.

"Where is Jean?"

The two women began crying and telling their husbands what had happened, which took a load from Paul's shoulders. When the women finally calmed down Paul's father asked, "Is this all true?"

"Yes. He died in front of me. He died like a man. No one feels this loss like I do, my life could never be the same without Jean in it. I never imagined my life in his absence, it was never to happen, and yet it did. I prayed for him."

"I am glad to hear that my son died well. I am happy that you survived, for that I will be forever thankful."

"For that, I will be forever miserable," Paul replied.

They sat around the table listening to Paul talk about he and Jean's exploits, they were quite impressed. Paul hated talking about it, but he owed them at least that. Paul started to cry, and then he told them about Luc. A young man, not much younger than they were.

"He died while Jean and I held him, we kept him

talking, we gave what care we could, but the wound was too severe. He passed while I was talking to him. Jean and I could not leave his body there, so we made a stretcher and carried him home to Marsal, to his family. That may be the thing that I am most proud of doing. All the good I've done has made me miserable."

Their parents were proud of them for their sacrifice. They continued talking well into the night. Paul had travelled a long way and he was tired, so he excused himself for the love of sleep. He slowly walked to the door of his old bedroom and put his hand on it, not to push it open, but to caress the past. A more serene time that had come and gone. He felt the white of the door, the familiarity and comfort that lurked inside. Paul pushed the door open and walked through it, closing it behind himself. Everything was the same as he remembered it. He laid down on the bed and started dreaming. He and Jean were playing as children in the lavender. They would pop up and show themselves then hide while the other tried to crawl to the spot where he believed the other to be located. Paul could not catch him, and eventually Jean quit showing himself. Paul was left alone running through the field, "Jean, Jean," but he never answered. Paul woke up in a cold sweat and laid there contemplating what he had just dreamed.

Paul missed those days of playing, fishing, and pulling pranks on their neighbors. However, it was not Jean that he was missing, it was his own life, with Jean. He knew from his dream that he could only chase after memories.

When Paul's father rose Paul was already awake,

sitting at the kitchen table with a cup of coffee. He poured a cup for his father.

"Will you be here when I return?"

"Yes. I will be here."

His father left and Paul continued to sit for another hour waiting on his mother.

"Are you hungry?" He heard his mother yell from down the hall.

"No, I am drinking coffee."

"Coffee is not breakfast," his mother said as she came walking into the kitchen.

"No. It is only coffee."

They sat at the kitchen table and talked for a while. Paul was holding back what he believed it was necessary to hold back.

"I must go by the bakery today. I have not smelled the bakery in far too long."

"Paul, the old baker died three months ago. He had a problem with his pancreas."

"I had no idea that there were ever any issues with his pancreas," Paul stated.

"He had chosen not to tell anyone about it. No one knew except he and his doctor. He missed you two very much. He always asked about you and Jean and was concerned for your well-being. It was hard on all of us to go so long without any word. It was difficult to not think the worst."

Paul had never known his name, he was always just the old baker, but they loved him. Without him there would not have been so many sunny days.

"I must go visit him."

Paul realized the loss immediately, another set of memories that he would chase indefinitely. Paul was far too young to hang his life on just memories.

Everyone that ever died in Briey was buried in the cemetery behind the cathedral, Paul knew where to go to find the old baker. He went into the field first and picked a bundle of lavender to place on the old baker's grave. He wondered how things might be different if he and Jean never left Briey, but that was a losing speculation. He slowly walked to the cemetery, thinking of what he would say to the old baker.

He found his grave on the left side, facing the back of the cathedral, and three rows from the front. He walked up and sat down next to the headstone marked Louis Ladeaux. His mother had told him what name to look for. He sat down beside the baker's final resting place and laid the bundle of lavender on the grave. He thought that he knew what he wanted to say, but he could not say any of it, at least not at that point. He sat there for hours just thinking and chasing memories. Once he started getting tired, he started talking.

"I have known you all of my life, still there was so much that I did not know. I am not sure whether I needed to know or not. Now that you are gone, I wish that I knew more. I wish that afterthoughts were not so easy. They are the least needed of recollections, and of the least use. Jean has died. I thought that I would tell you, since no one else knew either. I am sorry that I was powerless to do anything, but I am plagued with the possibility that I was not powerless. I just did not know what to do and I am sure that I still do not know. My life was good, I knew what I was doing and where I was going, I just did not ever think that I would have to go at it alone. Now my mind seems to be shutting down. I do not care about the things that I cared about. I am swallowing myself in pity, and it is making me feel lost. How do I continue with life and possibly find happiness?"

The words of the old sage came back to him, "You did what was right, so did Jean. You must forgive yourself. Or realize that there is nothing to be forgiven for."

Paul heard the words before and as true as they may have been the correlation between reason and his emotions was tenuous at best. He knew that if he were ever to get out of this depression it would be his own doing. Not the words of a wise man, but by strength of his own will. Strength of which he felt like he had none.

"I am sorry that I was not here, I am sorry that you left before I got back. I will always miss you and remember you for what you were to me."

Paul prayed that the old baker would have peace, and that he himself would eventually find it. Then he walked away heading back towards his home. It was not far away, but it felt like a long walk. The kind that your mind starts racing and then you realize that you do not know how you got from one place to another, no points of reference. Freedom from himself was all that he was seeking at this point, and it was the one thing that he could not have. He arrived at home to find that his parents were at the table waiting on him.

"You did not have to wait up on me."

"We were worried about you son," Paul's father said. "You have not been yourself since you came back."

"I was not myself long before I came back."

"What is it? Is there anything that we can do?"

"No. It is totally personal, there is nothing any one can do. I have seen and heard too much in my life. Some that will never leave me."

"Son. We can see your pain, and it only hurts us that we cannot help."

"Do not let yourselves be pained over my troubles. I will find a way to deal with them."

"I know that you will, I just want the best for my son."

They said goodnight and Paul went to his room. He pulled out his money bag and divided it in half, it was a lot of money. Paul had never had this much in his life. It did not make him happy, it did not make him sad. The point is that it did not make him at all. It was a tool with a purpose, and he planned to use it for this purpose. He had a dreamless sleep that night for which he thanked God when he got up that morning. He went to the kitchen and made a cup of coffee. Again, he was at the table when his father came in before he had to leave for the foundry. He poured his father a cup and his father sat down with him.

"Son, I was thinking, I can get you on at the foundry if you would like. Or maybe you intend to go back to school. What do you think?"

"Well, I have not given much thought to going back to school, it just does not feel right, not yet. I have seen and done enough doctoring to last me ten lifetimes. I really do not have any idea what I should do, but I promise that I will figure it out soon."

"Okay son, anything at all that your mother and I can do to help you let us know."

"Thank you. I will, I promise."

Paul's father left and his mother came out of her room and walked into the kitchen. She had been up listening to them. She carried a small bag with her. When she got to the table, she dumped the contents and spread them out on the table and arranged them in chronological order.

"These are for you Paul." It was the letters that had been sent by Michelle during Paul's absence.

"I meant to give them to you when you got here but I was overwhelmed, and it did not come to my mind until just now when I heard you and your father talking."

Paul began going through the letters and he did not stop until he had read every one. His mother sat patiently beside him while he read. There were over thirty letters from Michelle, the latest one was only two months old.

"I had written her back about four months ago, I told her that you loved her and that I knew that she loved you. She had been missing you dearly. I want to meet this girl."

"Maybe you will."

"Paul, what are you going to do about her?"

"I have not had to think about it until now. I love her, I have since I met her. I just cannot see my being any good for her when I cannot even be good to myself, she deserves much better than that."

Paul had thought about that, but not near as much as he should have. After the loss of Jean, Paul had spent many sleepless nights wondering if he could be blamed in any way. Even if he could not, he would still find a way to place at least some of the blame on himself. It prevented him from moving on.

"Paul, she deserves, at least, to hear that from you."

"Yes, I know, but I am afraid to face that, I can't possibly face her. I just don't think that I am ready for that."

"Son, you cannot run forever."

"No, you are right, and I am tired of running."

"You have always done the right thing, and I know that that part of you is alive and well. I have no doubt, as painful as it may be for you, you will always do the right thing."

"Thank you, mom. You always have said the right things to me."

"That is what mothers do."

When the conversation with his mother ended Paul went to his room and grabbed his money bag. He kissed his mother and headed out the door. He walked to the market. Paul needed the air and the expanse. As he passed the vegetables and the fruit, he could smell everything as a whole, or in his mind separate scents into what each part of the fragrance was. There were pears, apples, lemons, oranges, turnips, and every type of Mediterranean fruit and fish imaginable. Paul picked some up and put them into a woven basket. As he walked past the bread he thought of the old baker and how he missed him. Thoughts like this came to his mind all the time, he wished that they did not. The smell of the bread snapped him out of it, he grabbed two loaves and placed them in his basket. He continued, not at a hurried pace. He was enjoying the open-air market, air and expanse was what he thrived on. As he passed the meat, he bought some lamb and some pork from the local butcher, just a couple of small cuts. As he continued his stroll, he finished filling his basket. He bought a bottle of wine and that topped off his basket. He put the bag of money at the bottom of the basket and covered it up. Then he headed over to Marie's house. He did not want her to find it while he was there, he did not want her to think that it meant something other than what it was. He could hear her baby crying as he approached the door. He knocked gently and within a minute Marie was at the door.

"Oh my God, Paul?"

"Yes Marie, its me."

"The most awful rumors about the whereabouts of you and Jean were spreading through town like a fire. Some thought that the two of you were dead, some thought that you were still in med school. With Metz being in the hands of Germany now I doubted that that is where you were, so I had no idea what to think."

Paul did not want to tell her about Jean's death, but he knew that she would find out anyway, then she would wonder why Paul saw her and never said anything. News traveled extremely fast through a small village like Briey.

"Marie, Jean is dead. We were in a prisoner of war camp and he was executed."

Marie began to cry immediately.

"Paul, I am so sorry. I know what he meant to you.

I am so deeply sorry."

Wiping the tears away from his own face Paul said, "Thank you Marie. I am trying to live with it. This is for you," Paul said as he held out the basket to her. "I thought you and your little one could use it."

"Thank you so much," she said as she wiped her face dry. "Thank you for thinking about me and my child."

"I always will. Goodbye."

"Goodbye."

Paul had walked three blocks down when he heard Marie yell, "Paul, Paul." He ignored her and kept on walking. There was enough money in that bag for Marie to support herself and her child for a year. Paul did not want to have to explain himself. He was happy to be able to help her. As he made his way back home, he thought of the present instead of dwelling in the past. He could not remember when he had last done that, it felt good to him. For the first time in as long as he could remember he felt carefree, relaxed, this worried him.

The street was empty as he walked down it. They used to be bustling at this time in the early evening. There would be children laughing and balls rolling down the street, vibrant colors from the girls playing with banners, parents watching their children from out of a window, and gossiping with each other. All of that was gone, it seemed that the war changed not only individuals, but entire communities. The loss felt by everyone was tragic. France was still under Prussian occupation, at least until the war reparations were paid. Most towns escaped direct occupation, but the cities did not. Briey had escaped that humiliation.

Paul arrived home just as his mother was setting the table for dinner. His father was already seated so Paul drew a chair across from him.

"How was your day son?"

"It was good."

They all sat down and enjoyed a family dinner of roast pork, bread, turnips, and olives, and a bottle of Burgundy to wash it all down with. There was a feeling in the air that something was going to change. Paul's parents had no idea, or suspicion, but Paul had a good feeling.

After dinner they were having a cognac when Paul said, "I am leaving tomorrow."

"What? Where are you going?"

"Paris."

"Paris? For what reason?" His father asked.

"I have to go see about a girl."

His father sat there looking confused, his mother smiled at him. Before the sun rose the following morning, Paul was gone.

-14-

Paul had gotten so used to walking everywhere that he decided he would walk to Paris, the one-hundred ninety miles would take him about two weeks. He struck out from Briey heading west, towards Paris. Spread out in front of him was a purple field of lavender. As long as that was under his feet, he felt like he was home. He knew that it would not be under his feet for long, but he would enjoy the familiarity for as long as he could.

Walking for two days brought him to the town of Verdun. He was very tired, and hungry. The town had escaped the war, but as was the case everywhere, the people were left traumatized. There were still those that the war did not seem to touch. Paul could not understand how anyone, even if they had only heard about it, could not be affected. The town was not under Prussian occupation, but Paul had passed a small garrison about ten miles out. Verdun was spared the humiliation of an occupation by a distance of ten miles. As Paul walked into the town, he noticed that everyone behaved with a forced friendliness, hushed conversations, greetings with a guarded smile. The war had done that to almost everyone, every community. A thorough breakdown of trust. Paul had lost his belief in the inherent goodness of his fellow man, until he had met Max, but it was still not fully restored, it just took on more of a per person role. Paul found a small lodging house where he had found a room and a meal. The sun had not yet started to set, so after dinner Paul walked to the bank of the river Meuse. He sat on the shore wishing that the water could wash him away, that he could come up clean and new, free from guilt, free from his own torturous memories. He could not sit on the shore of the river and not think of Jean. It had always been a favorite pastime for the two of them, now Paul had to do it alone, it would always be alone, from now on. He closed his eyes and tried to let every thought be washed away in the Meuse. It began to gently rain, as the rain gathered on the fringes of his hair it fell into his face, mingling with the tears that were already falling from his eyes. The rain succeeded in camouflaging his feelings, or at least the outward expression of them. He feared that camouflage could become a friend. His life had never been so complicated, in a year's time things had changed that much, too much. The rain nor the river could wash that away. He made his way to his lodging, his bed was yearned for. When the sounds that accompany the first light cracked Paul was awake. He rose to the smell of bread being baked, but it had lost its luster, outside the realm of necessity. No baked good could ever measure up to his youthful appreciation for the old baker. That was nothing that needed to be dealt with, it was simply a fact. Paul grabbed his things and went downstairs, there was only one person up other than himself.

"Ma'am, I must go."

"I know. They never come here if the time to go never comes."

Paul settled up with her and bought two loaves of bread to take with himself. He crossed the bridge over the Meuse and continued west. He liked the feel of the soft grass underneath his feet and he would often spend the night in these soft green fields, the purple fields of Briey having been left far behind.

This was not a race to Paris, and Paul never even thought about why he was not in a hurry, but he walked along just as he had set out to do.

Four days out from Verdun, Paul came across a green, wildly sloping hill. It sloped at such an angle that on the downslope side Paul laid down and his body was in a position as if he were sitting up. Not wanting to walk up the hill on the other side, Paul fell asleep right there in that position. It was a surprisingly comfortable position for Paul to rest in. That was his last thought before the world turned black. Dreams escaped Paul that night, in the morning he was very thankful for that. Too long had dreams plagued Paul's sleep in recent months, it was refreshing to have a good night's rest without the unwanted burden of dreams. Paul sat where he was for a moment and enjoyed the beauty of this field and the rolling hills that seemed to flank him on all sides. He appreciated the beauty of this natural scenery until he felt like it was time to move on. Paul gathered his things and headed off over the hills. Paul enjoyed walking, taking his time, absorbing the beauty of the natural scenery that was all around him. There were few things in life that could truly put Paul at ease, pacify all his thoughts and feelings, beauty was one of them. Beauty, in all its forms; the countryside, fields of lavender, the green pastures that he used to lead the herd out into, and from the past, the face of his beautiful Michelle. He saw her in his mind and for the first time since Jean's death he felt a sense of purpose edging its way back into his life. He could not help but to smile to himself and thank God. He found his feet to be moving a bit faster in the direction of Paris. Now, instead of trying to get things off his mind, he was recalling Michelle in great detail, the love that he felt for her came flooding back into his heart and mind, without the guilt. In the recent past it was impossible for Paul to think of what there was to gain without being plagued by what he had lost. This had a paralyzing effect on Paul, it was like a festering wound that had begun to run, having never been given proper medical attention. He was beginning to realize these things for himself. The old sage had told him that when he came to grips with his own life, he would experience a rebirth. Paul wondered if this could be the beginning of that event. Yes or no, he knew that he had to get to Paris. He had been walking over hills and pastures for many miles, there had been no sign of a proper road. After several more miles Paul came across a path, he followed it until it became a trail, this he followed until it ended at the road to Chalons, which was just short of twenty miles away. Paul was almost half of the way to Paris. He set out on the road, passing many strangers as he went. He could tell that some came from Paris and some from Chalons. The women from Paris were wearing balloon dresses, as he and Jean had come to call them. The colors were so loud and vibrant that it appeared as if a circus was on the march. Paul found himself looking into the faces of all the women just on the small chance that one of them could be Michelle. None of them were, but the bright dresses and bonnets were fun to look at. The fear in the faces of those that had seen the recent horrors of Paris was not. Several people were also walking towards Chalons. Paul met an older couple along the road, they appeared downtrodden.

"Where are you coming from?" Paul asked.

"Vionville," the man stated.

"What brings you to Chalons?"

"We have a daughter living there. Our two boys were killed in the war. We just cannot stay there any longer."

"I am sorry to hear of your loss." Paul said, without volunteering any further information.

"So why are you going to Chalons?" they asked.

"I am actually going to Paris to find a girl that I

had fallen in love with before the war."

"I hope you find her. Love has a way of mending any wound."

This was a saying of true wisdom, and Paul knew it, but he was yet to acknowledge it. The three of them walked together for a while, mostly in silence, but when someone had something to say, they would say it.

As the sun was setting in the sky in front of them you could almost see Chalons, it appeared out of the sunlight like a mirage. Perhaps it was a mirage, but it was enough to keep Paul going.

"We will rest here for the night, and you?"

"I will continue," Paul said. "I feel an urgent need to reach Paris."

"May God go with you and help you find what you are looking for."

"Thank you," Paul said, as he continued his journey west.

By mid-morning Paul had reached Chalons. The city was bustling with activity, there were street vendors plying their wares. An old lady was selling jewelry while a young girl next to her was selling vegetables and housewares. Prussian soldiers could be seen on street corners or marching down the streets in a single file line. They kept to themselves, for the most part. There was a language barrier that aided this. The Prussians did not speak very much, and the French were glad of it. After having been thoroughly beaten in this war they held on to as much animosity towards the Prussians as they could muster. War was a bitter rival of all mankind. Paul made his way down the street avoiding any contact or conversation with anyone, he needed a bed. Such lodging he found down one of the many side streets, he needed rest. He slept through most of the day and well into the night. When he arose, it was still very much dark outside. He decided to take a stroll. He got up and put on his pants and shirt and then he set off walking. Not sure of where he was going, he just continued to walk. He walked through the streets of Chalons, past the women of the night that tried to distract him with their feminine charms, he never even turned his head in their direction. The gamblers hunched over their bets in the dark alleys, dogs barking loud from their desire for scraps, and the runaway orphans barking even louder from their desire for the same. All Paul could think of was to keep on walking. He walked until he found himself on the bank of the Marne, the same spot that he once stood with Jean. There were no tears in his eyes, only a pleasant memory of standing on the shore with his best friend. Paul was surprised that it did not drag up pain or the thought of the suffering that he had endured at the hands of those memories. The memories were his, he knew that they would always be there, he just needed to sort between the good ones and the bad ones. To recall pleasant memories at will was a gift, as was the ability to suppress bad ones. It was hard to stand beside the river and not think of Jean, and it was hard to think of Jean and not become saddened.

The sun broke over the water and made it glisten like gold. It was a beautiful thing to see, it was glowing like treasure. Suddenly Paul did not mind seeing it by himself. It lost no beauty whether Paul was alone or not.

The river carried no recollection of who basked in its beauty, or who did not. It was worth all the treasures of Europe. After spending many hours on the shore of the Marne, Paul made his way back to his room. He sat down on his bed and turned over in his mind his next move. He wanted to make it to Paris as soon as possible. Then he became extremely nervous about seeing Michelle again after so much time had passed, perhaps her situation had changed. It was quite possible that she had met someone else, she was a beautiful young lady and she would only be alone if she wanted to be. Paul hoped that at that moment she still wanted to be. Paul had walked about eighty miles in a week's time. He was tired and he knew that the rest of the journey would take at least another week on foot. He had grown weary of walking and he decided that he did not want to do it for another week. It was in his mind now to reach Paris as soon as was possible. He went to the waterfront to enlist the services of a riverboat captain, there were none available. It would be two days before a boat would be available. Paul figured that that would still cut his trip in half, so he decided to wait. The day was long and filled with boredom, it was inescapable. He could have attended a play or a cabaret, but his heart was not in it. If he were to enjoy such entertainment, he wanted it to be with Michelle. He could imagine a happy life with Michelle, but he could not see a happy life without Jean. Although he had gotten his emotions somewhat in check, his memories of Jean would still surface, when they did it very much saddened him, very much against his will. Paul found a place to eat, down one of the side streets, with little difficulty, as there was no shortage of said establishments. He had a simple meal of meat and bread with a glass of wine. He could afford a much more extravagant meal, he just did not see the need for it. The following morning Paul made his way to the waterfront. There were still no boats available, but Paul had little else to do. He enjoyed the company of the river, so it was not burdensome at all for Paul to spend his day there. He watched the people walking along on their way to no place special. He took notes of things like their fancy dress, or their plain dress, as well as their superficial conversations. He did not do this to judge, judging people was not a part of his nature, it was simply to entertain himself, the days boredom required him to do so.

When the late afternoon arrived, Paul went back to his room. He packed up his things in preparation for his departure the following day. He did not sleep very well that night, his mind kept dwelling on what he should say to Michelle. He had not had any communication with her since he was still in med school in Metz. There was a certain amount of fear in him of what their meeting might bring, but whatever it was he knew that he would have to face it. He had reached the point in his own mind that he had no choice. There were too many emotions that he would have to answer to.

Early the next morning Paul got up and went to the cathedral in Chalons, there he prayed for his loved ones that had passed away. He also prayed for safe passage to Paris and a favorable outcome when, and if he met up with Michelle. The last time that Paul had been in this cathedral he was with Jean, that fact did not escape his attention. Paul left the cathedral and headed down to the waterfront. When he arrived there were still no boats that were available to take him to Paris. He sat down and waited for a boat to become available, he would wait all day if he had to. Paul had already decided that if a boat did not become available by that evening then he would set off on foot. Fortunately, early that evening a boat arrived that was bound for Paris. Paul paid his fee and boarded the boat, he was asleep before it ever left the dock. The boat set out just before sunset and began steaming up the Marne. The rumble of the engine woke Paul up shortly after dark. Paul walked toward the wheelhouse until he found the captain.

"Kind sir," Paul asked. "When will we arrive in Paris?"

As the captain turned around, he recognized Paul, and Paul recognized him.

"My young doctor friend, how are you?"

"I am fine. It is good to see you again captain."

"How is your friend? The two of your names has escaped me."

"I am Paul, my friend was Jean."

"Was?"

"Yes. We were thrown into a prison camp during the war. Jean was executed."

"My God, why?"

"He and I were forced into giving medical attention to wounded Prussian soldiers and officers. When they refused to allow us to treat the French soldiers, which were dying around us every day, I refused. I was beaten and thrown into general population. Jean continued to treat them. One day a Prussian officer that was under his care died. Jean was accused of murder and was executed."

"I am sorry for your loss. It is hard to believe that a life so young and so full of promise can be so carelessly discarded, stolen so easily."

"It is a loss that I do not know if I can overcome. How did you get over the loss of your wife?"

"I have never, nor will I ever get over the loss of my beloved. Time has passed and that helps to ease the pain and the self-pity caused by her absence, but I do not wish to ever get over her. She and I both loved the river, we would sit on its shore for hours every day. That is why I came to work on the river, it reminds me of her and the love for each other that we shared. I have no desire at all to ever forget her, but time alone has helped me to deal with her loss. Now when I think of her, I can smile."

"Jean and I loved the river as well. Every time I do something that the two of us used to do, I cannot help but think of him and become saddened."

"You will always think of him, but you will not always be saddened by it. Time will pass and then you too will be able to think of his memory and the times that you had together, and you will smile."

The words of the mariner made Paul feel a bit better because he believed them to be true.

"Now," the mariner asked. "Are you on your way to Paris to find a beauty?"

"Yes sir, I am."

"How is she?"

"I do not really know for sure. I have heard what

has went on in Paris. We have not communicated since before I was captured. It has been about a year. I have a letter that she wrote to my parents a few months ago, and I hope that she is still at the same address."

"Son, you are off on an adventure. I envy your youthful vigor."

"I just hope that I can find her, and I hope that she still loves me."

"Hope is a great thing. The realization of that hope is even better. I am sure that you will be fine, regardless of the outcome. Think of what you have already endured."

"Even if I cannot find her, even if she has moved on?"

"Yes. Even if."

Paul took his leave of the captain and walked to the bow of the boat. He was pondering everything that the captain had said, he was undoubtedly a wise man. His capacity for love amazed Paul. The river had become his wife, and gladly so. Paul was beginning to understand that. It never diminished his love for his wife, it allowed him to bask in it.

Paul strained his eyes to look upriver, he imagined that he could see the lights of Paris, and that somewhere within those lights Michelle was waiting for him. He missed her dearly, and if nothing else, he wanted to see her again and make sure with his own eyes that she was happy. He agreed with the captain though, no matter the outcome his life would continue.

The boat arrived in Paris the following evening. Paul was both elated and terrified, but he was also brave enough to face whatever the outcome may be. There was a time in the prison camp that Paul felt like whatever happened, happened. This was both brave as well as stupid, but part of that stayed with him. It was that, and love, that gave him the courage to press on.

As the boat pulled up to the wharf Paul found the captain helping the other passengers to disembark, Paul began helping too. When the last passenger was gone Paul shook the captain's hand and said, "It has been an honor of my life to know you. You have inspired me and given me courage."

"No, I did not. These are things that you have always had, I just helped you to find them."

"Be that as it may, I will never forget you."

"Nor I you."

Paul walked down the old wooden wharf until he reached the cobblestone walkway. As he looked down at the cracks in the stone, he thought about how old they must be, centuries. He was at Pont Morland and wanted to get to Notre Dame. He felt the need to pray and get God's blessing in his search for Michelle. Not as much for the search as for the outcome. He took a carriage to the bridge at Pont St-Louis, from there he walked to the cathedral. He stood in awe of the massive structure. Remembering that the only other time he had been there Jean was with him, he cracked a small smile, it was far better than the tears that he probably would have shed had the captain not helped him put things into perspective. He had lost the only love he had ever known, yet he could talk about her with all the love that he had for her and it made him happy just to have ever loved someone like her. He walked inside and knelt in one of the pews close to the altar. He felt that the closer he was to the altar the better the chance of his prayer being heard. He knew that was ridiculous, but he felt the need to be closer, so he was. He prayed for Jean, the old baker, Max and Nicole, and lastly that he would find Michelle, and find her well. He left the cathedral with a renewed sense of vigor. As it was late in the evening Paul headed to the Hotel de Ville to get a room for the night, he would begin his search for Michelle in the morning.

He left the hotel early the next morning on his quest to find Michelle. He had an address from a letter that she had sent to his mother a few months earlier, twenty-two St. Germain. He took a carriage to that part of town, he did not want to walk having done a lot of that over the past year. He arrived and stepped out of the carriage, his heart was beating out of his chest. His thoughts were running amok. Maybe she would not recognize him, maybe she would not care. He decided that he would face whatever the situation entailed. He made his way up the stairs to room twenty-two and stood outside the door for what seemed like a lifetime. Finally, he mustered up the courage to knock, no answer, he knocked again, and then again. After about five minutes an older lady stepped out into the hall.

"Can I help you?" she asked.

"I am looking for the girl that lives here."

"No one lives here."

"There was a girl that lived here a few months ago."

"Ah, Michelle. Such a sweet, quiet girl."

"You know her?" Paul excitedly asked.

"Yes, she left about two months ago."

"Did she leave an address?"

"No. I am sorry, but she did not."

Paul felt his heart begin to sink. How could he possibly find her in a city this big, if not for blind chance. There was no one that he knew that he could inquire about her residence. He began to wander the streets of Paris looking for her, he had no belief that he would ever find her in this city. As he scoured the city he would pop into the theatres, cabarets, even the opera house, just to ask if anyone might recognize her, no one did. As he walked along the boulevard, he was approached by a beautiful woman that asked him if he would care for any company.

"No," he said. "I am afraid that I am not very good company right now."

"Perhaps you and I could change that."

"Thank you, but I have no real interest in changing that."

"Well, if you just want to talk, we could find someplace quiet. Down by the river perhaps."

"That's it!" Paul yelled. "You are right. Thank you so much, down by the river, yes."

"You are welcome, is there anything else I can do for you, anything at all."

Paul kissed her on her cheek and said, "No."

He turned away from this unknown proposition and ran as fast as he could down to the shore of the Seine, the same place that Paul, Jean, Michelle, and Claudia had sat when Paul and Jean had told them how much they loved the river. Paul found a bench and parked himself on it. He just sat there watching the river for hours. He became oblivious to the comings and goings of the hundreds of people that passed right by him. He did not pay attention to their fancy dress or to their mannerisms. He only had one thought on his mind, and he had decided that it would not come to fruition. As he got up to walk away, he turned around and there she was, standing a short distance behind him, crying.

"Michelle?" Paul asked, already knowing that it was her, but not believing it. "Michelle, is it really you?"

"Yes," she said between sobs. "I thought that I may never see you again."

"Michelle, I was never going to let that happen. I love you." Paul said.

"And I love you."

Paul was ecstatic, what he thought would never happen, happened.

"Why did you come back after so much time?"

"I came back for you, only for you. I want you to marry me."

"I have always wanted to marry you."

"Will you come with me to Briey?"

"Yes," she said. "I will go anywhere with you."

The following day they were on the train headed to Briey. Paul told her all about his internment and Jean's subsequent execution. She told him about the closing of the art school, the rise of the Paris commune and her belief that Claudia had been executed for her part in it.

"Are you going to go back into medicine?"

"I am not sure if I can ever do that again."

"I will support you whatever you decide to do, as

long as we are together." Michelle said.

"Do you have any idea how afraid I was that I would not find you, or that I would find you no longer in love with me?"

"I shared the same fears. No one knew where you were. I had been going down to the river every day for two months. I remembered how much you love the river, I thought that it might be the only way that the two of us may find each other. I don't know if I thought it would work, but I knew not doing it wouldn't."

They spent many hours on that train catching up with each other without any tears, they were unimaginably happy to finally be together. Paul felt as if he had finally reached a place that he had been trying to get to all along. He could feel happy for himself without feeling guilty about the death of Jean. He became blissfully unaware of the troubles that were all around.

They arrived in Briey and made their way to Paul's parent's house. His parents, especially his mother, as she had read the letters Michelle had sent, were beside themselves with excitement at getting to meet their future daughter-in-law. Michelle and Paul's mother hit it off immediately. They spoke about the letters that Michelle had sent and the hope that they had given them. Paul's mother cried until her eyes were dry, she loved this young woman that was to be her son's wife. She was happy to help with wedding plans and harbored no thoughts about Michelle not being right for her son. Life, after so long, had finally seemed to have set itself aright.

Paul took Michelle around the village and showed her all the things that had been, and that were important to him, the old bakery, which remained closed, but it had been recently purchased. They went to the cemetery to visit the tomb of the old baker. Paul told Michelle how much he had meant to him and Jean. He took her to Jean's parent's house to meet them.

"Paul, my dear, where have you been?"

"I had to go to Paris to get my bride," he said while smiling at Michelle.

As she reached out and took Michelle by the hands she said, "She is absolutely beautiful."

"Thank you," Michelle said while trying to keep from blushing.

"When is the wedding?" Jean's mother asked.

"It is in three days. There are still a couple of people that I want to be there, and I have to get an invitation to them."

"It means a lot to me that the two of you are there, I only wish Jean could be there too."

"Paul, there is no need for you to get upset about that, we have all come to terms with our loss. He is in God's hands now."

The following morning Paul rode north to Malmedy, Michelle stayed in the capable hands of Paul's mother.

That evening as Paul approached Max's farm Nicole saw him coming and ran to him screaming for her father. Max came outside and saw the object of Nicole's excitement, he ran towards Paul as well. Paul had dismounted and was running towards them, he caught up with Nicole first.

"I missed you Paul, but I knew that you would

come back to see me."

"Of course. Was there ever any doubt? I will never go a long time without seeing my Nicole. You look like you have gotten so big."

"No Paul, I am still just a little girl."

"Maybe now, but you will not always be."

Max approached and gave Paul a big hug. "I am so glad to see you back Paul. Please tell me that you are staying. Half this farm belongs to you, you have to stay and take care of our investment."

"I will, but I have one more thing to do that I would like for you and Nicole to do with me."

"Sure Paul, anything you need, anything at all."

"Come back to Briey with me for my wedding."

"You found her," Max yelled. "You found her." Max grabbed Paul and squeezed him tight, bouncing him up and down with Nicole screaming her happiness and excitement for Paul was overflowing. "I knew that you would. God blesses the vigilant."

"Would there be room on the farm for me and a wife?"

"You know there is, and whatever we have to do to make it more accommodating, we will." "So, you two will come back with me tomorrow?"

Before Max could answer Nicole was asking, "Can we daddy, can we please go?"

"Yes dear, we will definitely go."

"Thank you, Max. Your presence means everything to me."

"Thank you for riding up here to invite us, your wedding is not something that we want to miss."

"After the wedding we can all come back here, then we will get to work on the farm."

"Sounds good."

The following morning, they all headed out, Max and Nicole in a carriage and Paul riding just ahead of them. They were well prepared for a trip that would take all day and into the evening. Paul thought about going to the sight where the old sage had laid down to die, or to the remains of the internment camp that he and Jean had been, but he knew that it would be impossible to retrieve their bodies for a proper burial. He prayed for those two all the time, and still he wished that he could have done more.

-15-

That evening they all arrived in Briey. Paul took Max and Nicole to his parent's house where they were all introduced. Max was incredibly happy to meet the people closest to the man that he considered to be a hero. He told them the story about how Paul had saved Nicole's life from an exploding shell. Everyone, including Paul's parents were in awe. It was a story that Paul had not told. He did not like to talk about such things, he was not a braggart, nor did he see that as a cause for arrogance. If he had wanted that kind of recognition then he would have thousands of stories to tell about saving the lives of his countrymen, as well as Prussian soldiers. The stories that he talked about were few and of his own choosing. Even when he spoke of Jean's death, he still only told the necessary part, namely, that Jean had been executed. There were some things that Paul knew that he would carry with him until he died, but he had come to terms with that.

Everyone was so happy for Paul and Michelle, the entire village showed up for the wedding which was held in the field of lavender that he had spent so many of his days enjoying. It was a simple ceremony. Paul had insisted that Max and Nicole stand at the altar with him. He looked over at his mom and dad, his mom was crying, and his dad looked at him with his face beaming with pride. He always knew that his son would do something special, and he had, but he believed that much more lay ahead for Paul. Jean's parents were both crying, they lost Jean, but Paul had always been theirs too.

There was a big feast after the wedding. The entire town needed some levity, memories of the war were not that far behind in everyone's mind. This festive occasion was something that everyone had needed, especially Paul and Michelle. Michelle adored Nicole and was pleased that they would be living on the same farm.

Paul's dad approached him and asked what he was going to do. "Are you going to finish medical school? You could work at the foundry or on your uncle's farm."

"No dad, I am co-owner of a farm with Max in Malmedy."

"Son, you have endured a lot and have come a long way since. I want you to know that I love you and am so proud of you."

"Thank you, dad, now I must leave for Malmedy to see a man about some cows."

When the festivities had died down and everyone was headed to their own homes, Paul, Michelle, Max, and Nicole headed off to their farm. Life there became extremely rewarding, Michelle loved the country. In a short amount of time Michelle had become pregnant. Paul never saw himself as a father, now he saw himself as nothing else. Their child was born, a boy, in the fall of 1874, they named him Jean. Paul would often walk the fields with his son. It felt wonderful to walk and talk with him, and to say his name, Jean. His son was the only person that Paul told everything about his namesake. He loved his son dearly and treasured every moment with him. Michelle was an attentive mother and wife. She adored their son and treated Nicole as if she were her own, and she dearly loved Paul.

The next decades were full of peace and prosperity. The farm flourished and they all did very well for themselves. It was a perfect place to raise a child. There years were fun and fulfilling. In the year 1890 Max took ill with an unknown malady. Later that same year Max died. Paul and Michelle raised Nicole as if she were their own child, they loved her dearly and she loved them as if they were her parents. In 1894 Paul and Michelle gave her away in marriage. She had a baby boy in 1896, she named him Paul. He grew to be a fine young man. He wanted to go to medical school like his grandfather. To get up enough money on his own he joined the army, much against the insistence of Paul and Michelle. Paul's memories came flooding back to him and how much he despised war. In the year 1914 the Great War broke out across Europe. Paul and Michelle prayed for their grandson to escape this catastrophe. No one knew that this war was going to be unlike anything that the world had ever seen, and it carried with it the promise of more stolen lives.